Unlikely Neighbours

GILL BUCHANAN

Unlikely Neighbours

First Edition Published in Great Britain 2013

ISBN 9781849143639

© Copyright Gill Buchanan

www.hensdancing.com

All rights reserved. No part of this publication may be reproduced, stored in or introduced into any retrieval system, or transmitted, in any form, or by any means (electronic, mechanical, photocopying recording or otherwise) without the prior written permission of the publisher.

This book is sold subject to the condition that it shall not, by way of trade or otherwise, be lent, resold, hired out, or otherwise circulated without the publisher's prior consent in any form of binding or cover other than that in which it is published and without a similar condition including this condition imposed on the subsequent purchaser.

This book is a work of fiction and any resemblance to actual persons, living or dead, is purely coincidental.

To Chris, Clive, Gayle, Jim and John for your words of wisdom, 152 coffees and 119 pieces of cake that went into the writing of this novel.

Chloe

'The High Life Shop offers Executive Club members the chance...'
 ...for some peace and quiet at this unearthly hour in the morning? Perhaps not. If only I'd recharged my lap top last night, I could have finished that report for Robin and emailed it through as soon as we land in Brussels. That would have impressed him. But that's the trouble isn't it? When you get home so late your mind is muddled. The client meeting up in London didn't finish until seven and *then* they insisted on going for drinks. By the time I reached my little house in Lodge Lane I was shattered. A cup of tea and ten minutes of Graham Norton and the next thing I know it's morning and I'm throwing a strange selection of garments into the all too familiar overnight bag. I've got an awful feeling I'm going to be wearing navy blue underwear and a cream see-through blouse tomorrow.

 The cottage is great. Pity I don't spend more time there. Robin really stitched me up with this European Fund. Not your average fund where you baby sit a few blue chip stocks, oh no! This is your bloody impossible *Green* European Fund.

 'We pride ourselves in offering these funds to investors with a concern for our environment,' he spouts at every available meeting. Of course he doesn't mention that these so called concerned investors are absolutely livid if they don't make any money. Hence I'm charging round Europe trying to find some profitable Green companies. I'm seriously thinking of rewriting the definition of green. How about, must have a green logo? Or, must wear green uniforms made of biodegradable cloth?

 Before, when I was on the UK desk, the furthest I ever went was Ireland and you can do that in a day. No badly coordinated underwear in those days. But I was married then. Being married goes down well with the City toffs. A mark of respectability it seems. Means they can ask the obvious question when they can't think of anything else to say; 'and how's the husband?' I don't think they ever remembered his name.

Then there are the unwritten rules around having children; most essentially the need to book the date for the happy arrival to fit around meetings. Caesarean only, of course, none of this time-wasting natural method. Wednesday 4th March meeting in London. Thursday 5th March check emails before hospital appointment to give birth. Friday 6th March ensconce nanny and work from home. Receive large bouquet of flowers courtesy of Fitch and Kemp with delightful message re: looking forward to seeing you back in the office on Monday.

But of course *I* didn't want children. That was the problem. If only David hadn't assumed I'd come round to the idea. Is having a child something you can make assumptions about? To think he let me go through the whole wedding thing, the meringue dress, the ridiculous fuss, the family fall-out … only to discover that he wanted a child more than anything in the world. More than me.

And then Robin put me on Europe. Well, it took my mind off things, he was right about that. The work load increased exponentially and of course any spare time is spent travelling. Luckily the change of job came with a pay rise and I was able to afford a cottage in this lovely village. Must be twenty miles out of London but more importantly only twenty minutes from the airport. All the neighbours are very endearing in their own ways; not the sort of people you're going to become bosom pals with. Although I don't think the same can be said for the guy who's just moved in next door. He seems to have a complete disregard for the rest of us. You see the lane is postcard pretty but very narrow and so you have to be considerate about where you park.

The other morning I was booked on the 7.45 to Paris and I'd cut it really fine having got to bed very late the night before. In the rush to get ready I broke a nail as I struggled to get my case down the narrow stairs. They were looking so good as well, all the same length and I'd actually put a pale pink polish on them for once so I was really miffed. I flew out of the house only to realise that the new guy had left his humungous classic Bentley right in the middle of the lane making it impossible for me to get out. Anyway, I'm pretty grumpy first thing at the best of times and this just tipped me over the edge. To make things worse when I first knocked on his door, he just seemed to ignore me! I knocked again. And again. Eventually he appeared, still in his dressing gown, God knows what he does for a living! And he stood there like I'd just landed from space or something. Eventually he managed to speak. 'Good Morning. Can I help?' Well, by then I was ready to scream at him.

'Yes! You can move your car out of the way!' I said rather too loudly.

'Oh, is it in your way?'

This man has to be stupid as well as thoughtless.

'Of course it's in my way! You'd struggle to get a wheel chair past it!'

'You've got a wheel chair, have you?'

'No! I haven't got a bloody wheel chair, but I have got a car! You know one of those small unassuming things that you can park without causing chaos!'

'Really, there's no need to get worked up. Just a few minutes and I'll move it right out of your way.'

'A few minutes! A few minutes and I'll have missed my flight!'

'Oh! Right well this is most inconvenient. As you can see I'm not even dressed for the day. But I suppose needs must. I'll just get some shoes.'

He sauntered back into his house like he wouldn't notice if a tsunami hit him. It was a miracle I caught that plane. So, looks like I've got an arrogant, selfish buffoon living next to me. Still, with this job, I'm hardly ever there.

It's when I *am* there that's the problem. I put all my time and energy into work and as soon as I have a free weekend I find myself wondering what on earth I'm going to do. All my friends got married when I did and they've stayed married and have kids now. So when I pick up the phone to them on a Saturday morning and say casually, 'fancy supper tonight?' I get something on the lines of: 'What *this* Saturday as in *today*?' There's no attempt to disguise the horror in their voices. Then they continue, 'The thing is, John's gone to pick Jamie up from football and then Sophie's off to the birthday party of one of her best friends and then Tommy will arrive for his sleep-over with Jamie. And then of course we're up early to get Tommy back home to his family before we all go to church.'

I feel exhausted just thinking about it. But as I put the phone down the quiet stillness of the cottage hits me. I'm lonely.

Alex

Beautiful isn't it. The way there's a light dusting over the neck and the deep plum of the wine is held in the green reflective glass. I invited some friends round the other evening, just to admire it. It was a bit of a moving-in party. When Miranda suggested we actually opened it and drank it I said,

'You've got to be bloody joking! That's a 1988 Châteauneuf-du-Pape. Probably cost you a couple of hundred to get that uncorked in The Ivy.'

Of course she was straight back with the obvious question,

'So when *are* you going to drink it?' She looked at me with those come to bed eyes she's got. I could almost feel her claws sinking into my chest. I had to put her straight.

'Miranda, darling, I'm sure the right occasion will present itself one day.' I said knowing it would be with someone a bit more special than this little lady.

Harry and Debs seemed quite happy with the rather cheeky Sauvignon I served up with the Indian take-away. Oh, and of course, Miranda had to make one of her quips about my kitchen only needing the occasional dusting as it's never used. Still she's got the most impossibly lovely body. It's worth putting up with her silly comments, for a while, anyway.

You're probably thinking I'm some sort of wino with all these bottles around me. Not true. I just love a descent drop of wine occasionally. Well perhaps a bit more than occasionally. But I never drink on Mondays because I play squash with Freddy. Good of him to keep it up, even though we don't work together any more.

But anyway, when I first saw this little cottage whilst I couldn't help wondering where the Chesterfields were going to go, I just loved the fact that it has a cellar! My wine collection seems to be one of my only indulgences left. Well that and the

Bentley. Of course Miranda sniggers every time I tell her it's a *classic car*.

'Clapped out banger' she retorts.

What does she know? So here I am in my cellar surrounded by some of the most exquisite wines you're likely to find in this neck of the woods I shouldn't wonder. I've spent quite a bit of time down here already, considering I've only just moved in. I find it quite soothing when the negative thoughts start rolling and things are getting on top of me. It helps me contemplate, well, life, I suppose. That's why I decided to put this old leather chair down here. You have to climb over a couple of cases to get to it but somehow it creates a place where I can just be. Miranda would probably call it meditating. It's got to be better than that counselling lark. I can't believe they even suggested it; the insensitive bastards.

Of course upstairs is a bit cramped. I had to get rid of a lot of stuff. Kept one of the Chesterfields but the other went up to the parents at The Manor in Hinchcliffe. They haven't seen this place yet and I can't imagine them here somehow. It's just so different to my old place. When I talk to them about it they go quiet and change the subject. Christ, I'm still their son, despite everything that's happened!

Now I'm spending a lot of time at home and with this lane being so narrow and the houses so close together I can't help but notice the neighbours. The woman next door at number one looks interesting. Pretty. Blonde. Slim. My type altogether but I've only seen her twice. Both times she was in a suit, carrying one of those overnight bags on wheels. I think she must be an air hostess. My motor was in her way early one morning and so she knocked on my door. It was one of those irate, loud knocks that goes right through you and made my espresso go down the wrong way. And I must admit I had a bit of a hangover. Harry came round the night before. Bordeaux I seem to remember. Fruit slightly too ripe for my liking but don't worry I've made a note. 1998. A year to avoid in that region in future. Anyway by the time I'd tightened the old dressing gown to make myself decent and got to the door she'd virtually banged it down.

'Can I help?' I asked. I thought that very polite of me after her causing an unnecessary scene.

'You can move your bloody car out of my way! I need to get to work!' she said or something like that. The great thing was that even as she said it, our eyes met, and the most beautiful smile crept across her face. Of course she wiped it off immediately, but I knew, she fancies me.

Bit late for cups of sugar now. Perhaps I should offer her a free driving lesson. Anyway, two attractive people living next door to each other; let's face it, it's just a matter of time before we end up in bed together.

Then there's a single mother at number three. At least I've not spotted a husband. Smallish child, about so big. What would that be? Two? Boy, I think. I do feel sorry for her but I just don't have the constitution for all that wet stuff; nappies, sick, crying. It's just not for me and I'm worried if I get friendly with her she'll ask me to baby sit. It would be like putting an elephant in charge of a Ming vase. Disaster.

It's certainly a world apart from Oakdene. The houses were so far apart you only met your neighbours on the golf course, by accident. Then if you beat them you invited them round for drinks or vice versa. And depending on how much you wanted to win, you might just think well if he's got some decent wine, why not?

They all turned out to be the same types. The nouveau riche. Unhappily married in large modern houses, strangely full of antiques. Then I thought that it was the fact that they were married that was the problem. Now I'm not so sure.

Freddy still talks to me about the office even though it's been a year since I left. He always asks if it's OK first though.

'Do you want the gossip, Alex old chum, or shall we talk about sport?' he says.

Frankly I'm not that interested in sport and I can't help being curious about how the survivors are getting on. You see it was a year ago when they got rid of me. Greycoat Investors, the largest fund managers in the Square mile. Fifteen years I had been managing their global portfolio, rather well, though I say so myself. They called it a restructure. The fact that I'm forty nine was obviously against me even though since the age discrimination act they had to dress it up as something different.

'You see Alex, the thing is Alex, your particular role, and well it's just not part of the new structure, the way forward.'

So what does that make me part of? The way backwards? Certainly feels like that. From big fat salary every month to watching my capital disappear like quicksand. From middle class suburbia to banging my head on quaint old beams. I can hear the estate agent now,

'This delightfully small cottage with abundant period features set in a delightful village is very convenient for all amenities. No chauffeur required.'

But this is it. My new life. Lodge Lane.

Becky

Jack, he's such a love when he's sparked out. He really seems to like it out 'ere in the sun. Course I 'ave to 'ave the hood up to protect his skin from those UFO things. There was a great big hole in it. The hood I mean. But I've patched it up as best I can. Apart from that, it's not bad, even if it is from the charity shop.

You'd think it was way too noisy for him out here. You see we're near the High Street and it's a busy little village. But still he's only two. Not a care in the world, the little mite.

Couldn't believe my luck when I landed this place. There ain't many homes I can afford in posh areas like this and the last thing I wanted to do was to 'ave to move to a rough area. I don't mind telling you as soon as I stepped foot in the lane I fell in love with it. Couldn't believe how everyone bothered with roses and hangin' baskets and all sorts outside their houses. Makes it look like a proper lane. And I just thought I could be happy here. Start again.

Ever since they took the junction out on Eddie, he's not supposed to come near me. The woman at the refuge said he had to stay 100 metres away from me and Jack. Or was it 100 yards? Anyway it's the same difference.

I think the woman who owns it took pity on me. She seemed to like me. And when I explained that she needn't worry because the council would be paying most of my rent anyway, what with me being on benefits; well, she didn't bat an eyelid! Must be pretty bright see 'cos it makes sense really, if you've got someone on the social then you're always goin' to get your money. In the end, that is. The council are ever so slow. But you know most landlords take one look at people like me and run a mile.

'Don't you worry dear,' she said. 'I can tell by just looking at you that you won't cause any trouble.'

And before I knew it she was asking me about Jack, as if that was that. And that was a whole year ago now.

There was loads to do when I moved in because they'd been this old couple in before and it was all flowery wallpapers with that awful furry stuff. I couldn't live with that. But don't worry I checked with Mrs Barnes. That's her, my landlady. She said I'm sure you'll make it better. I like Mrs Barnes. So, I just had to wait till the white paint was on offer at the DIY shop, buy a couple of buckets of the stuff and get to work. But I knew it was gonna take ages to get rid of the wallpaper. Luckily, Chloe, two doors down, lent me a steamer thing that sort of blasts it off. She said she'd hired it for a week, but only needed it for a couple of days at the weekend, so I could have it the rest of the time. She poked her head into my front room and said, 'your need is greater than mine, darling.' Don't think I've ever been called darling by a woman before.

And you know I thought it was ever so kind of her and I really wanted to give her some cash for it but I'm always skint. Luckily I've been able to give her a few flowers since. She seemed to really like that. Would you believe, she gave me a big hug. I like Chloe. I've decided that. Pity she's not around much. She's got some flash job up in London managing posh people's money. But get this, she goes flying off to Paris, Holland and even Germany, all sorts of places. She says it sounds glamorous but it's not. My life doesn't sound glamorous and it's not.

It's funny to think we both live in Lodge Lane. She probably paid for her house with cash. 'What's that Mr Estate Agent? Quarter of a million quid? No problem. I'll get me accountant to arrange that now.'

I suppose there's no point in having a big place if you're never there. And she doesn't seem to have people round much. I see a cleaner go in once a week; has her own key.

Then there's this new bloke who's just moved in next door. He seems to have quite a few mates going in and out. And he's got this posh old car, you know one of those that's so old it's become expensive again. He parks it right in the middle of the lane like he's got no common sense. Doesn't bother me of course. I don't have a car. I can't help thinking how bloody brilliant it would be to have one, though.

Alex, his name is. I found that out the other day. You see I was just putting Jack in his pram so we could go up to the shops to buy a tin of baked beans and there he was. Seemed quite happy to say, 'Hello' and to introduce himself. He squeezed my hand ever so tight when he shook it.

'Alex Minter-Kemp,' he said. Or at least I think that's what he said. Strange surname I thought. And even stranger he felt the need to tell me. 'Becky,' I said. I still haven't decided whether or not I should go back to the name I had before I was married and I wasn't going to let this man rush me into a decision. So I just left it at Becky, for now.

He didn't look at Jack though. Everyone looks at Jack and says what a love he is. Not this fella though. And then I noticed him fidgeting from one foot to the other like a school boy wantin' to wee but not wantin' to say anything.

'You alright, love?' I asked.

'Splendid. Lovely to meet you. Got to dash,' he said. And that was it; he was off in his car. Sounded like some sort of bird being strangled. I was almost glad I was walking.

Anyway, paintings one thing, then there was the floors. The carpets downstairs smelt so bad that you almost choked every time you came in the house and I was worried that the bad air would get in Jack's little lungs. So I peeled a bit back and underneath was this dirty wooden floor but I know you can make them all shiny again so I was really pleased. Anyway I heaved all the carpets up and threw them outside. Then I thought I better ring Mrs Barnes and tell her. She didn't seem too bothered. She said she'd get the council round to take them away. Anyway, this place must be lucky for me because next thing I know Chloe's seen the dead carpets out on the lane and she's knocking on my door. It turns out she's decided to do her floorboards as well even though they're not half as bad as mine and she's hiring an electric sander for a week. One that looks like a hoover. And guess what, same deal, she only wants it at the weekend. It came to me that I had plenty of flowers in the garden so I'd give some more to Chloe and then not feel so bad about the sander.

It was really hard work, but they came up a treat. Jack didn't like the noise but luckily the nice couple next door at number four had him for a bit to stop him crying. He's good as gold really. I got rid of all the dust and varnished them and for ages it made me smile every time I looked at them. But you know what, as soon as I'd finished I thought, garden next.

It's alright here, don't get me wrong. People seem posh but they have good hearts, even Alex next door maybe. I love Jack to bits, but you know it's really hard bringing a kid up on your own. There's never any one to look after you. And somehow even though you're not on your own, you sort of are. 'Cos babies, beautiful as they are, well, you can't tell them you've had enough, 'cos you've had a bloody awful day and you just wanna cry.

George

Sheila's gone to choir practice. She always goes on a Wednesday, after Sainsbury's and before dog-walking. Not our dog, of course. I wouldn't have a dog but various people around the village who are out at work all day and need their dog's walking and well, it's Sheila who takes them. It means she earns a bit of money and as she tells me frequently, 'I need to get out of the house each day.'

Then she usually refers back to 'that' time when she was on the tablets. No sooner has she mentioned it again and she's suddenly cleaning the house or doing the washing-up or off out again.

Of course we don't need the money. My pension from the force is quite enough for our needs. Twenty five years I did. Twenty five years, then I said to Sheila, 'that's it, I've had enough'. And the great thing about the police force is that you can retire early and collect your pension. Well, I'm happy as Larry. Sheila thought I'd be bored; that I wouldn't know what to do with myself. She said,

'You'll be under my feet all day.'

It's funny though, thinking back, it was about that time that she had her funny phase and the Doctor put her on the tablets. Still we've been married for 27 years and we've had some good times. We've had two children and our daughter, Wendy, has two herself now and they don't live too far away. We manage a good holiday every summer and we've got this place on Lodge Lane really lovely now what with a bit of hard work and a bit of saving up to get the right furniture. We've just finished the spare room; put a new bed in there, the old telly from downstairs and I put some shelves up. Sheila wanted the walls pink. I said it wouldn't be my choice. She said she would be spending more time in there than me.

Of course I prefer it out here in the shed. Even in the winter it's not bad with my comfy chair and the heater on. Sheila says she doesn't know how I manage to spend so much time in here doing nothing. But, of course, I'm not doing nothing, although the time does seem to fly, especially if I've got a flask of tea with me. Anyway, I've got all my tools in here and my workbench. I'm just putting together this dolls house for Wendy's first born. I can't wait to see her face when she sees it.

I've also fixed a few bits in the house. The toilet roll holder from the bathroom works properly again now. I said to Sheila, 'Have you noticed? Have you noticed what I've fixed in the bathroom?' She just raised her eyebrows and carried on hoovering.

The woman at number one is very nice, even though she's divorced. She doesn't say why and we don't like to ask. But she's been on her own all the time she's been here and that's a few years ago now. She's an attractive looking woman so I'm not sure what's going on. Sheila keeps saying why don't we invite her round for drinks or something but I say what would she want with us? We don't know much about fund management; that's what she does, you see. It's funny, Sheila seems quite keen to invite the neighbours round but when I suggest we have some old friends round for dinner she makes excuses and starts hoovering again.

Then there's Becky, poor dear. Her ex-husband knocked her about by all accounts. It's shocking what goes on. Now there's one who doesn't hide anything. She was round here one afternoon, we had a cup of tea together in the shed, and well the woman can talk for England. Sheila loves looking after Jack but Becky doesn't ask very often. I don't think she can afford to go out. I think Sheila misses having the children around the place.

Just last week we acquired a new neighbour at number two. Alex, his name is. Said he was between jobs when I met him briefly and asked him what he does for a living. Anyway, he certainly looks well off enough with his flash car and there's quite a few posh looking types rolling in and out of his cottage. Makes you wonder, doesn't it?

Still, I'm going to paint the inside of this doll's house, now. Thought I'd use some of the pink left over from the spare room. And it will be nearly finished then.

I haven't a clue what time it is but Sheila usually comes to find me when lunch is ready.

Sheila

This is the best part of the day. Doesn't matter what the weather's doing or how heavy the ground is, I love trudging through the fields with the dogs running round, all excited. The first time I did it I was quite nervous; I thought I might lose one. But now I'm used to it and the dogs have got to know me and, well, it's wonderful! We always go across Hosey Common, through Paddock Wood and back along by the river to the village. It was Doctor Knox who suggested I took up walking. She said it would be good for me. At the time I thought she was mad. I just couldn't imagine wandering around fields on my own. It was Chloe who came up with the idea that I walked dogs. There'd be lots of demand for it, she said. She's a lovely woman, Chloe. She doesn't even have a dog herself, but she thought of it, just for me. She's very intelligent; got a high-powered job in the City.

Anyway, it turns out that the doctor's right. There's something magical about being in the fresh air with my walking boots on, making my way across muddy fields, hearing the sounds of the trees, the river and the dogs panting as they run up to me with a stick between their teeth. Yes, this is definitely the best part of the day. Even when it's pouring with rain, it's like I can laugh my cares away.

And I actually earn money doing it! George doesn't ask about it, he says it can't be much, so I decided to save it up. Goodness knows what for, but sometimes I think of the money mounting up bit by bit and it makes me smile. I opened a savings account with the building society in the village and I just pay it in each week. I told them not to bother posting my statements as it's just as easy for me to call in for them.

George is happy with his pension. He says it's quite enough for our needs what with the mortgage being paid off and the house exactly as we want it. And he says we'll never want to move except maybe to a bungalow when we're too old to get up the stairs. We're rationed to one holiday a year and George is quite content with that.

    I sing in the choir too. Me, sing! I quite enjoy it. I had no idea I could sing really. George said he hears me when I'm dusting and it's not bad but I never thought I was good enough for a proper church choir. It was the vicar who suggested it. Funny, he just seemed to know that it would help me. I didn't even go to church before George retired. He won't come, of course. Says he doesn't believe. Well I haven't a clue what I believe, all I know is, it gets me out of the house and when I'm in the church it's like it casts a spell over me and I feel all peaceful and calm inside. Makes me quite emotional sometimes; I find myself with a tear in my eye not for any particular reason. And you meet some lovely people. We have a cup of coffee after the service on a Sunday so there's a chance for a natter. I like meeting new people.

    Of course, I can't stay too long. I have to get home to cook lunch for George. It's his favourite meal of the week, Sunday lunch. It's the only time I call him from the shed and he comes straight away. He always wants beef. Sometimes I do lamb for a change and he says,

    'I like the lamb, Sheila, but I prefer the beef.' I don't say anything.

    Sometimes my daughter Wendy comes with the children and then it's really nice. A proper occasion; worth cooking a special roast for. David, our son, has only been once since he told us he prefers men to women and that was a disaster. George can't accept him the way he is.

    'There's nothing like a mother's love for her son,' Mrs Jacobs said after church one day and she's right. But I didn't tell her about his preferences in the partner department. Well, she didn't ask.

When they announced on the telly that people like David could sort of get married by having a civil partnership ceremony, George turned over and watched Anne Robinson instead even though he hates her.

There was a time when I thought to be married was the most important thing in anyone's life but now I look around me, at all my friends and neighbours, and somehow, it doesn't seem important at all.

Chloe

I decided that Nourriture Verte was the perfect stock. They seem very keen to invest heavily and their products seem to be going down well with their customers, and let's face it, this is a growing market. Anyway I've bought 250,000 shares at €5 each. What a ridiculous price! I must be mad! One and a quarter million of my clients' money spent on some potty French firm.

The worst bit was when Robin decided to congratulate me with this big smirk on his face:

'Well done Chloe. Interesting stock!' he said virtually breaking into a laugh while he looked straight over my shoulder at James Henderson, current star fund manager at F&K.

'Well, sink or swim, eh Chloe?' he patted my back before heading straight for James's desk. When I first worked here that remark would have been enough to keep me awake worrying, night after night, for weeks. Now I just about manage to contain the worrying to daylight hours. But I do have more faith in myself, or is it some higher being that I sort of believe in? Anyway I try to let go and more often than not it works and the stock comes good. After all, this job is just a posh version of putting money on horses. You win some, you lose some.

I'm in the office most of this week; just one quick trip to Chantilly, just outside Paris, on Friday. So I've been home a couple of evenings and I couldn't help noticing that the chap next door has started parking his car at the end of the lane, where it's out of my way in the mornings. Anyway, it must have been about 8.30pm the other evening and there was a knock at the door. I thought it must be Becky wanting a favour or maybe one of those teenage boys selling dusters so I was really surprised to see my neighbour standing there holding a bottle of wine.

'Alex Minter-Kemp,' he said quite simply holding his hand out as if I hadn't screamed at him last week.

'Thought it was about time I formally introduced myself.'

Without time to think what to do I reciprocated. And as I met his hand with mine, he shook it firmly as if he knew a limp hand shake would score him nil points.

His blue eyes lit up and he had such a lovely smile, I couldn't help smiling back. But then I felt a little foolish so I stopped. It was then he handed the bottle of wine to me.

'Just to say sorry about the motor; being in your way, I mean. Silly of me really when you have to be getting off at all times in the morning to get to the airport. I assume it is the airport you're off to?'

'Well yes.' Still in shock I found myself examining the label on the bottle of wine and suddenly wondering if that was rude of me, as if maybe it wasn't worth drinking.

'Bordeaux Superieur 2000. Rather good year. I hope you like red? I could always pick a white out if you prefer?' he said.

'No, no red's lovely, thanks. But you shouldn't have. It was just that I was in such a hurry to catch my flight that day.' I thought about inviting him in but then I would have to open the wine and I might never get rid of him. I always try to get to bed early in the week. God that sounds so boring doesn't it? What kind of a life do I lead?

'Fancy a coffee?' I heard myself saying almost like an out of body experience. His face lit up momentarily but then he looked disappointed.

'Coffee?' he seemed to question.

'Yes, coffee.' I didn't want him to be in any doubt now.

'Lovely,' he said running his hands through his blonde hair as if this was the least lovely suggestion he'd heard all week.

'Oh, you've got this place rather nice,' he said as he walked in and I wished that the magazine on the sofa wasn't opened at the article headed 'Are you having trouble reaching orgasm?' Then to add humiliation to embarrassment he picked up the self-help book on my coffee table: 'Surviving Divorce'. He actually had the audacity to flick through a few pages and renounce with pure flippancy,

'Not something I've ever had to bother with.'

I decided to make the coffee very strong, for him, at least.

'Milk and sugar?' I asked.

'Just black,' he said and I thought, even better.

He sat down on the sofa next to the magazine and didn't even flinch. I imagined he was probably taking in the article as I made the coffee. I was quite low on Pure Columbian so just tipped what was left straight into his mug and selected decaff for myself.

'Unusual to serve espresso in a mug,' was all he could say after the first sip. But then a grin appeared on his face and he went on to say, 'you must show me how you make it some time.'

Why did this man make we want to throttle him?

'So, how's the airline business?'

I couldn't work out why he thought I would know anything about airlines. Frankly, I know nothing as they certainly don't fall into the Green arena but I decided to make polite conversation anyway.

'I expect they're struggling what with all the low price competition and then all the criticism they get for destroying the planet.'

'Yes, you must be concerned about your job?'

'My job?' Now he'd completely lost me. 'I tend to fly at the front of the plane.' I tried to explain. 'Well, I have to arrive fresh or I couldn't function.'

'Ah. You work in first class. Must be much better than at the back. Do you get to sample the champers?

'What are you talking about?'

'You are an air hostess aren't you?'

'An air hostess?' Suddenly I wished I'd opened the wine.

'I'm a fund manager for Fitch and Kemp up in the City.' I said rather too angrily.

'Oh! Dreadfully sorry. Seeing you with that bag going off to the airport, well, I just assumed.'

Ah, so woman with suit and trolley bag equals air hostess! I'm not sure what expression adorned my face at that moment but he did spend some time back tracking while I tried a couple of deep yogic breaths to calm myself down.

'God, I'm so sorry,' he said finally and the strange thing was he did look mortified. Seemed like the weirdest of reactions for someone so arrogant. He reached for the magazine beside him and gently closed it. His face looked grey.

'You OK?' I was really annoyed that I was feeling sorry for him but this was some reaction.

'Lived here long?' he said forcing a smile.

We talked about Lodge Lane and I couldn't help noticing that he manoeuvred around questions about his past and how he ended up here. I must admit he doesn't exactly fit in. Finally he heaved himself up from his chair and said, 'Bathroom upstairs, I take it?' As he went up the stairs I had a dreadful thought. I remembered I'd washed my laciest black wonder bra and matching thong knickers earlier that evening and they were now hanging over the bathroom radiator right next to the hand towel. I decided maybe I should put the house on the market first thing tomorrow. Why do I insist on making sure I'm wearing my sexiest underwear just because I'm meeting up with Andrew from the Far East desk? I can't help fancying him even though he seems completely disinterested in me. As if he is *ever* going to see my underwear! I was almost smiling at myself when Alex returned. His spirits seemed suddenly elated.

'Fancy dinner some time?' he said so casually it took me a while to register what he meant.

The answer had to be no. Of course I don't want to sit through dinner with this prat, even if he is my neighbour.

'OK.' I said, and even as I did, I just assumed I'd find some way out of it that would be less embarrassing than saying no to his face.

Annoying thing was, despite the decaffeinated coffee, I couldn't get to sleep that night.

Alex

I popped round to Chloe's the other evening. Saw her car in situ, selected a decent Bordeaux from downstairs and sauntered round there. Thought it would be good to get to know her over a decent drop of wine. She was a bit cagey though. Kept me on the door step for a bit and then offered me a coffee! I don't think I've ever received a decent bottle of vino and then offered someone coffee. Obviously still upset over the Bentley, but I've been really considerate this week; I've been parking it at the end of the lane out of her way. I was beginning to think I'd caught her at the wrong time of the month, I know it affects Miranda like that; once she poured half a bottle of Chablis over me! Premier Cru as well! What was the woman thinking! Not only did I have a dry cleaning bill to contend with I was a bottle of Chabbers down. And for what? Silly woman stormed off making the whole evening a bloody disaster.

But you know once inside Chloe's place there were definitely some clues around. The woman's obviously desperate for sex, she's even reading about it in some magazine article. Not only that but I find out she's divorced and has obviously had a bit of a hard time of it. Seems to me that her and I getting together for a bit of a fling would be ideal.

Actually, I had a quick read of the magazine article while she was making the coffee but it was all a bit technical for my liking. Anyway, never had any problems myself in that department. I'm sure I could teach her a thing or two.

I must admit her place is rather lovely. Has a really cosy feel and was very tidy. Mine still looks like the removal firm have just dumped my possessions where there's a space, probably because they have. I keep noticing the microwave at one end of the Chesterfield and the bathroom cabinet at the other and thinking I must do something about that. I'll sort things out tomorrow. I want this place looking good if I'm going to be entertaining lady friends. Mind you I suppose Miranda's been round a couple of times already. I think I better cool things with her; could get tricky with Chloe on the scene.

Trouble is with Chloe, she's got my old job. Well, not literally. But she's working across the square from my erstwhile place doing virtually the same thing. Came as a bit of a blow, if I'm honest. I suppose it was because, without that kind of blunt reminder, one can get through the day not really thinking about what's gone on over the last year or so; but knowing she's jetting round the globe sizing up potential investments for her fund every time she goes off, well, it's not easy.

Still I tactfully managed to avoid telling her about my past. Gave her a bit of a story about deciding to pack in the rat race and explore different options. Even had myself convinced it was some sort of life plan as I spieled it all out.

After a year of going for jobs in the City, the prospects in that neck of the woods are looking pretty grim. It's a small world, the world of investment and word gets around. As soon as they know you were pushed, they're just not interested.

I have been up to the old Square Mile a few times. Managed to persuade the odd senior bod to see me for an informal chat. I use the word informal so that they know they've got the obvious get out clause:

'Sorry, old boy, you're just the sort of material we would be looking for, if we had any vacancies.'

Somehow I think if we get chatting and I manage to impress them with my knowledge of the global investment market, and believe me there's not much I don't know about it, then they might just give me a break.

The last time I went up there it was to see Richard Carnegie of Carnegie Birch and Bayley. I was kept waiting for over half an hour having to listen to the receptionist cry down the telephone to her girlfriend about some beastly boyfriend turning up to meet her parents for the first time at Eastwell

Manor in Lycra shorts. Seems the chap was a keen cyclist but had had strict instructions to wear chinos and a blazer. Well this girl certainly didn't see the funny side of it. Couldn't help thinking the poor chap was better off without her. Not that I've ever felt the need to wear Lycra shorts, but hardly seems to be some sort of offence.

Finally Carnegie's secretary turned up and didn't even bother to apologise for keeping me waiting.

'Mr Carnegie will see you now,' she said with the warmth of a slap to the face. To think I sunk a fine Bordeaux with the chap in Corney and Barrows only 15 months ago and now it was out with Dickie and he was Mr Carnegie to me. At least he had the decency to shake my hand.

'Alex, good to see you. How you doing old chap?'

'Excellent!' I lied.

'Good, good,' he said knowing I was lying.

'You look well.' he said.

This was getting ridiculous.

'Really?' I didn't bother to hide my surprise too much.

'Now, how can I help you?'

That question hurt. He knew damn well why I was there. In the brief telephone conversation we'd had after weeks of my trying to get hold of him, I had told him I was still looking for a job. Still I kept up the pretence.

'Just keen to know what's happening here at CBB and if there are any areas you think I could help out.'

It sounded so lame but I'd tried everything over the last six months; going for the jugular, avoiding the subject almost entirely and pretending I really was interested in their wives' conservative club fete, and something in between. Nothing worked.

Dickie shuffled around in his seat. If there's anything I've learnt about body language, it is, that this means, get lost you're making me uncomfortable.

'As I'm sure you know Alex,' he'd dropped the old chum bit so this is the left hook to the jaw coming, 'Stocks are still climbing out of the last recession so we've all had to tighten our belts. Expenses aren't what they used to be.'

Of course I know all this. But the fact is they're all recruiting younger blood. They have more energy and cost a lot less. It's got to the stage now, a year down the line, when the very thought of another informal chat fills me with loathing. The longer you're a reject the harder it becomes to answer the inevitable question.

'So Alex, what have you been up to since leaving Greycoat Investors?'

'Ah, well, been bone idle mainly, just sold my enormous house to move into a two up two down; it's great because now I've got enough money to eat and potter about for a bit longer. And you know it's not all bad; getting blotto on the remains of the wine collection helps to numb the feelings. Of course, I've spent a fair amount of time having futile conversations with people like you who just see me as a nuisance. All things considered it's been a bloody fantastic year!'

What a mess. I've got to stop feeling sorry for myself. But what am I going to do? The capital won't keep me in Veuve Cliqueot forever. And I certainly couldn't end up like Becky, relying on the state, no doubt, and living on baked beans.

I was sat down in the cellar just the other day, and I was thinking up plan B. If only I could do plan B I'd be OK. Of course, this is something which doesn't rely on employers, big corporates, anyone like that; and it's really good for me and earns me just enough money for a reasonable lifestyle here in Lodge Lane. You know, able to drink the odd bottle of fine wine, afford take-aways, keep the Bentley running and enough to take a lady out for dinner every now and then. Well, a man's got needs you know. Yes, trust me, that would make me happy. I just haven't worked out what plan B is yet.

I asked Chloe out to dinner. She's damned attractive and I thought it would do us both good. She did hesitate but frankly by then I was beginning to think the woman must be a bit frosty. Anyway, she did say yes, but we didn't arrange a date or anything. I think the element of surprise is the only way to go with this one. Maybe I'll order an Indian take-away, open a cheeky Sauvignon and call on her.

Becky

The old people that lived here before me, well, they were pretty old-fashioned when it came to decorating but they must 'ave known a thing or two about gardening. You see whilst it's narrow, it goes back a long way and there are some incredible plants in there. It's great the way different plants come up at different times like they're replacing the ones that have just died. It must have been all planned out at one stage.

The first time I looked at the place, must be about a year ago now, it was full of big colourful blooms and Jack just gawped at them as he tottered round, a bit unsteady on his feet then. He couldn't resist touching the petals and squealing. And I thought this is so lovely I'm goin' to have to learn to keep it this nice. You see when I was with Eddie we could only afford a flat and so the best I could do was window boxes. I always had them lookin' nice but Eddie used to get angry and say they were a waste of *his* money. Then there's Mrs Robinson. She lives just up the road from the last place but one, and her garden is huge and truly magnificent. I always feel better when I go up there. You see I used to clean for her to get a bit of extra money and she'd always be in the garden busying herself and she didn't mind me goin' out there. I'd make her a mug of tea and she'd say:

'Are we doing the tour today, Becky?'

I used to feel a bit weird when I went up there. Like it was a different world. What you might call surreality. I felt sort of tingly all over. I suppose because I was away from Eddie and all the trouble he caused, and Mrs Robinson, well, she treats me right.

Anyway we used to walk round the garden and she'd tell me about how all the plants were doing. She knew the names of them all, the Latin as well. Wow! I used to think, but would you believe it, I know a quite a few me self these days!

Dear Mrs Robinson; She must be 82 by now and she still does her own garden. She used to get up from what she was doing, might have been planting or pruning, and she'd put her hand in the arch of her back and lean into it and say,

'My Becky, that feels better.'

I'm not her Becky, but I wouldn't mind if I was, so I've never bothered to say anything about it. And she smiles at me and her face is all wrinkled, from the gardening so she says, but she has a lovely smile. One of those smiles when you're wondering what someone's thinking, cos it looks like they're thinking ever such a lot. And I think she knows. About Eddie I mean. I think she just knows but she doesn't say anything 'cos she is clever enough to know it's best not to. Last thing I want, is to be thinking about that rat bag, while I'm in me dream world.

One day I went out there, with the tea as usual and she said, 'would you like to help me today, Becky?'
Well, of course I said yes without hardly thinking about getting back to Eddie in time.

Anyway she was plantin' bulbs in one of the beds, tulips and daffodils, I think they were and we planted away. She seemed happy with her own thoughts and I was havin' to concentrate hard so as not to get it wrong and the time just past ever so quick. But when I got home Eddie was waitin' for me.

Anyway when I moved into Lodge Lane and I saw this garden, I decided, straight up, I'm goin' to keep this garden as nice as Mrs Robinson's. Of course, I'd learnt the basics from her and I've read a couple of books in the library, 'cos actually I find it ever so interesting, but that's it really. I just do what I think's best for the little loves. Seems to work; most of the time.

When I'm feeling a bit down, you know, everything's getting on top of me, what with Jack throwing a tantrum and one of his toys breaking – and he seems to just know I can't afford a new one – well, I usually say,

'Let's go out in the garden Jack and see what's occurring.'

And he looks at me with his big blue eyes and before you know he's found his shoes or maybe even his little red wellies. Works like magic. And it just seems to do us good gettin' out there and gettin' muddy.

The Spring blooms are brilliant right now. I've got these stunning tulips, all stripey they are, red and yellow. Then there's the baby dafs, the freesias that smell so gorgeous and the Hyacinths that are the colour of the sky on a clear blue day. Me and Jack, we keep starrin' at them like they've just suddenly appeared and we didn't have to do all the hard work to get them there. And we stare as if we have to take in all the beauty because next thing you know they won't be there anymore.

I watch the Chelsea Flower show on the telly every year and I think how superb it would be to go there. Just once, you know, to se e all those amazing creations. All the people milling about look dead posh but the ones that actually do the gardens, well, they look pretty normal to me and I could see myself there, with Jack of course, manning some pretty brilliant garden we'd done. Jack would have to understand that it wasn't for playin' in but just for show. I'm sure he'd get the 'ang of it. Or Sheila from next door could 'ave him but really if I made it to somewhere like that I'd want him with me 'cos it would be a special moment and I'd be ever so proud. Don't suppose me and Jack could ever afford it. Not even to go there. It's things like that that get me down. Things that I really, really want to do but there don't seem to be a hope in hell of ever doin' it.

Some of the time I manage to forget I haven't got any money. I go off in to this dream world. Pretend I own the bloke next doors' Bentley and me and Jack live in a big mansion and throw a posh ball every now and then just so as I can wear me diamonds. All famous people come, of course, like Girls Aloud, Kaiser Chiefs and Back Street Boys. Oh and of course a few film stars like Jude Law and Kate Winslet. Yeah, they all come and we drink Champagne all night and waiters all dressed in black and white serve those little bits of food they do in Marks & Spencers.

Anyway, usually I'm well away and then I realise Jack's pulling at my sleeve and we don't have anything in for tea and I'll have to go up the road for a tin of baked beans again or shall we splash out and get the one with sausages in as well.

It's all very well havin' a nice garden, but however amazin' it is, who's ever gonna see it? Apart from me and Jack, of course, and don't get me wrong, we love it, but sometimes I can't help thinking; what's the bloody point?

Sheila

They look so small in my hand. A bit like Junior Disprin but of course they're adult white, not childish pink. It's hard to believe something so small could make such a difference. The doctor said it's the dog walking and the choir just as much as the tablets and she says I'm doing really well. But I'm still not sure I want to give them up. George thinks I ran out and I don't take them anymore. He noticed the empty packet one day and said,

'Now, look, they're all gone and you're feeling so much better aren't you dear?' And before I had chance to say anything he was off. 'You're like a new woman. You won't be needing any more of those. I know we're both agreed it's best not to take them unless you really have to.'

It's like he's mapped out the next bit of my life without even considering what I think. I'd already put a request in for a repeat prescription at the surgery and I was picking up the next batch after choir.

What I like about choir is that the people just accept me how I am. They don't know what I was like before the tablets because I wasn't involved with the church then. I suppose they just think I've suddenly decided to find the Holy Spirit. Funny that, when actually I've come here to lose George rather than find God. Mrs Jacobs also sings in the choir and she talks about her husband like he's a five year old child.

'He always chooses the wrong tie, I have to tell him. It's the blue stripey one for the solicitors and the red one for family gatherings. And he's all fingers and thumbs so I have to tie it for him. After breakfast, of course, or you can guarantee he'll get marmalade on it. I keep hoping that Lakeland will bring out a wipe-clean variety. After all they produce some marvellous things in that shop.'

It's funny George and I seem to get through life without

worrying about ties. Still, you don't need a tie on to sit in a shed.

Anyway we're singing, in four part harmony. I'm soprano, that's just the tune, so the easy bit and it sounds lovely when it all comes together. Mr Barry, the conductor, allows us a quick smile at the end if we get it pretty much right. 'Good.' He says ever so quickly. 'Next!' And everyone shuffles their music sheets around wondering which is next.

George mentioned our annual holiday the other evening.

'It's April and we're still not booked up! We're always booked by February. I can't think what's happened this year apart from the tablets which I know has been a bit of a setback. But then surely a holiday is precisely what you need!'

'Perhaps we should go a little later this year, you know out of season. Isn't it cheaper after the school's go back?' I tried to make it seem alright.

'Well yes, but you can't rely on the weather.'

I couldn't help remembering last year when it proved to be the wettest July on record. Somehow you need the sun for St. Ives.

'So what shall we do then?' George seemed irritated and I did feel sorry for him.

'Leave it with me.' I said and somehow thought I'd find a solution that would suit us both even though I hadn't got a clue what that was.

I spoke to my son David the other day. Sunday evening it was. George was actually out. He'd gone up to the Grasshopper with his friend, Arthur, for a pint. So I was really pleased when David answered the phone.

'Hello.' He always sounds a bit abrupt at first.

'Hello David, it's your Mum here.'

'Oh, Mum! How's my super Mum? Still guardian to all the village dogs and providing life and soul to the church choir?' He always makes me giggle with his interpretation of my silly little life.

'Yes, I'm pretty good thanks.' I haven't told him about the tablets. I wouldn't mind actually. I know he'd understand. But George thinks the less people that know the better.

'Good. Good.' He sounded thoughtful as though he was trying to work out what I wasn't telling him.

'And you son. Tell me what you're up to?'

'I've decided on a complete life change and I've bought an antique shop.' He said it so plainly it took a while for it to sink in. I was about to say 'what about your job in sales?' when I thought again and heard myself say calmly,

'That's wonderful David.'

'Thanks Mum.' He said and I think he was quite choked up.

'In *your* village, actually.' Again the words were so innocent, the meaning so heavily loaded with connotations I didn't even want to contemplate.

'I see.'

'Do you think Dad will mind?' I wanted to laugh, cry, run naked through the streets and hide under the spare room bed all at once.

'I think he'll be surprised.' I managed carefully and realised I was pouring myself a brandy.

'I am, who I am, Mum. And I want to be near you. I know you've had a tough year and it would be nice to be able to pop round without it being a big deal. You see I've got the flat above as well. It's 'The Green Antiques' on the Green, of course.

I've been in there often. The French woman who currently owns it is dark, slim and graceful. She always looks fashionably smart. I often have a wander round the shop. They have some beautiful things. To think that my son is going to own it, is quite amazing. If I could have just stopped imagining George's reaction I could have relished the moment my son decides to move back to his village and set up home and shop. It has the makings of a blissful life. If only it could happen without George knowing. I suppose I would be living a double life. It's funny but it almost feels like that already; he always asks about choir,

'How did it go dear?'

'I really enjoyed it today,' I might say.

'Good. That's good,' he says wondering off to the shed not wanting to know any more. He never asks about the dog walking apart from:

'All back safely?'

At first, when I worried about that very thing, it seemed kind that he asked. Now it's just like ground hog day. And yet the walks are always different, the sunshine and the rain, the leaves on the trees might be rustling or still. Will I have Mrs Poodle's snowy white Geraldine or will it be Mr Alsation's dribbling Rex?

I don't know what to do about it, this double life I seem to be leading.

'Will you be living in the flat above The Green Antiques on your own?' I asked David and I was surprised at myself but it was the question that was searing a hole in my brain so it just came out. I needed an answer, the 'yes' answer.

'No. Actually Mum I've been with Nigel for quite a while now. I know I've not said much but I never know what to do for the best. But you see just because I'm gay doesn't mean I don't want someone special in my life.'

He stopped there and there was quite a long pause and in the end I decided to forget about what George would think.

'I'm really pleased for you son.'

'Oh, Mum, you don't know what that means to me.'

The tears burst from my eyes and I took another large glug of brandy. I don't even drink brandy, normally.

David was like an excited child telling his Mum he'd just found an unexploded World War bomb at the bottom of the garden.

'You see it's all because of Nigel that I can do this. He's got some capital to invest and, well, we've talked it through and decided that I'll manage the shop and he'll continue with his hairdressing career until it starts to earn us a steady income.'

'He's a hairdresser.' I felt really silly for stating the obvious but the words just fell out as if they had to.

'Yes, Mum. He works for a top London salon and goes all over Europe when the fashion shows are on. He's done Kate Moss's hair lots of times. Can you believe that?'

Somehow that seemed very believable.

'Good.' I said and wished I hadn't because I never want to sound like a disapproving Mum. And then I said what I really wanted to say.

'David, I'm overjoyed at your news and the thought of you being in the village is fantastic. I can't wait to meet Nigel. I know he'll be lovely. If he's your partner and you've chosen him then he will be lovely and we'll get on well.'

'Thanks Mum.' He interrupted me.

'But I haven't finished.'

'Can't we leave it there?' It felt good.

'You know your Dad's going to find this really difficult, don't you?'

'He's hardly acknowledged my existence since I came out. Even when I'm sat opposite him eating a Sunday lunch I wonder if maybe I'm invisible.'

'He finds it hard,' was the only explanation I had for that.

When I think about how I'm already leading a double life and doing everything I can to spend time out of the house and I still haven't booked the holiday I just couldn't face up to this right now.

'Who's going to tell him?' I asked him gently as if that helped.

'It'll have to be you, Mum.'

I popped the whole conversation with David and all its consequences into the outside bit of my double life and decided I'd just leave it there until it couldn't be there anymore.

George

The Grasshopper's always full of youngsters but you can get a decent pint and Arthur doesn't seem to mind. We usually find a corner in the back bar and sit and watch the pint settle until we take our first sip which is always the best sip of all and the only one you really remember. And then we can report in on the comings and goings of our lives.

Arthur knows more about what's what than I do, even though we're both living in the same village. He's on the Parish Council and goes to church and seems to be involved in every village committee going.

'I like to keep busy,' he says using the excuse that he had a demanding working life and now he's retired he needs somewhere to direct his energy. Me, I'm quite content with mending things and creating things in the shed. That's enough for me. And I need to be there for Sheila. I wouldn't want her coming home to an empty house after what she's been through.

Anyway, Arthur knew that the shop in the village, The Green Antiques, is about to change hands. Not that it's of much interest to me.

'Madame has decided to go to back to France.'

'Well I expect she misses her family.'

'Apparently she's sold to an English couple.'

'Well perhaps that's more appropriate for this village. After all we kid ourselves that we get on with the French, don't we?'

'I quite like a bit of French influence. Did you know most of the antiques are French?

'Never been in there, myself. Sheila has though; she seems to like it. Usually comments on how lovely the furniture is. Wouldn't look right in our house of course. We've gone for the modern look. Much more practical and I prefer it to old rotten furniture.'

'But you live in an old cottage, George.'

'Doesn't mean I want old furniture.'

'Mmm.' Arthur does that sometimes. Says mmm as if he's trying to agree but thinking something entirely different.

'Anyway maybe the new couple will bring new furniture, after all they've only bought the premises. Might even be a different type of shop, something useful, maybe, like a DIY store', I said.

' I doubt it somehow,' Arthur said.

'Well, whatever it is I wish the new owners all the best!' And with that we clunked glasses and had another sip.

Chloe

As the share price of Nourriture Verte plummeted, my heart sank and my body wanted to descend under the desk. It was all I could do to avoid the gaze of Robin, who definitely did know what was going on, and those of others who may have picked up on it. I'm never sure in these situations if it's my imagination or if there really is an eerie silence across the floor to accompany the demise of the stock. Eventually, inevitability caught up with me, and Robin planted a condescending pat on my shoulder.

'We all have our bad days, Chloe. Shame you went in with both feet. Over one and a quarter mill wasn't it? But still presents you with an interesting challenge. Now, of course, you need to think about what you're going to say to the investors.'

Not one of his most motivating ditties. I can't honestly say that I was left feeling empowered. No the message hurtling at me from between the lines, was Chloe, you're in the shit, get yourself out of it. Meanwhile James Henderson practically glows and we're talking halo not perspiration.

Davina caught me at the end of the day, spun me round in my chair and with her hands on my shoulders looked straight into my smarting eyes.

'Darling Chloe, share prices may go up as well as down and the same applies to alcohol levels.'

And with that I managed the first smile of the day.

Corney and Barrows had its usual vivacious atmosphere with the low level chatter and laughter interspersed with the odd manly bellow of a suited toff surrounded by clones massaging each other's egos. As I couldn't spot anyone that I knew, I at least had the pleasure of being anonymous in there.

'This should do the trick.' Davina poured ridiculous amounts of Pouilly Fume in two bulbous wine glasses and handed one to me.

'To all that is green!' she cried and we both laughed mainly as a result of hysteria.

'Green and rising,' I added to demonstrate that my sense of humour hadn't left me completely.

'Sounds dreadful, darling. Now only one rule for the evening; No talk about work. Tell me about your love life.'

'What love life?'

'This new neighbour of yours. Alex, isn't it?'

I had mentioned to Davina about Alex moving into the lane and the two disastrous meetings we'd had which has now actually become three.

'I'm not in love with Alex! Far from it. In fact he's got to be the most conceited, arrogant, commitment phobe I've ever met!'

'So, you fancy him?' she said as she leant back into her chair and made no attempt to stop the smile dividing her face.

'No I don't fancy him! He turns me on about as much as a luke warm cup of cocoa.'

'Just a bit then.' She grinned even more.

'Davina! Trust me! I don't fancy him!'

'He sounds quite romantic, quite spontaneous, calling on you like that to invite you round for a meal and a decent glass of wine.'

'Huh! A take away! Extra spicy Indian, sure to repeat on you! And with the sole intention of getting me into bed!'

'When was the last time you had a shag, darling?' I hate the way she cut to the chase.

'That's not the point.'

'No, you're quite right. This guy obviously can't cook, is very presumptuous about your desire to shag and despite having excellent taste in vino and lovely blue eyes; *your words, not mine*; he's not really what you're looking for right now.'

I decided that we needed a diversion.

'I fancy Andrew on the Far East desk, you know that.'

'Always a sucker for unrequited love! Anyway, I hate to tell you this.' Davina leaned towards me and lowered her voice, 'but I'm pretty sure he's seeing Chantal from Marketing.'

'But she's half our age! And she behaves like some sort of footballer's wife!' I screamed, half wishing the whole bar knew who I was talking about.

'Obviously his type, what can I say? The man just doesn't have good taste. Forget about him. Now tell me all about Alex.'

My heart sank. Our third and what has to be our final meeting, if that's possible while we are still neighbours, was no less than a calamity. In fact, I suspect Blair feels better about the Iraq war.

'Not much to tell really; bit of a disaster.'

'But he invited you round for supper, even if it was a take-away. Maybe he's just too nervous to cook for you at this stage. The evening must have had its good points. What did you talk about?'

'The wine was exquisite. He's a bit of a buff on that score. He's turned his basement into a wine cellar. Quite remarkable actually.'

'See! He was trying to impress you!'

'I suppose it was going quite well to begin with. Turns out he used to work up here.'

'No! Really! What's his surname?'

'Minter-Kemp.'

'Alex Minter-Kemp. Didn't he work at Greycoat Investors before that restructure?'

'Well, yes. He's a bit vague about why he left. I suspect he went when the new CEO came in and made a few changes. Must be pretty awful actually. I don't think he's worked since.'

'Oh gosh that's rotten. Still if he can afford to buy exquisite wines can't be doing too badly. Yes, I think I can picture him, blonde chap and I know what you mean about the blue eyes.'

The first bottle of wine slipped down rather too easily and before I knew it Davina was up at the bar ordering a second. I watched her as she sauntered up there, her Prada bag swinging from one arm; she has to be the only woman I know who can look sexy in a cardigan. Probably because her rather magnificent breasts mean that the buttons have no chance of reaching their intended homes.

Some ridiculously good-looking guy, he must have been half my age, beamed at me from across the bar with his perfect white teeth, fresh from the cosmetic dentistry chair no doubt. I managed to smile back but suddenly felt exhausted. At that moment Davina reappeared.

'You alright darling? You look like you need a pick-me-up. Here.' She administered more wine. I noticed we were still on the PF and thought in my tipsy state how good it was we weren't mixing our drinks.

I hated watching her face as she obviously thought we were getting to the good bit of the tale when really it was the part that made me wonder what's it all about?

'So, the crucial question, did you shag?'

I almost thought for a moment that it would have been better if we had and I'd maybe have had a smile on my face for a day or two and then put it down to experience, but we didn't.

'No. Somehow I wasn't in the mood when his girlfriend turned up.'

'Girlfriend! What do you mean?'

'We'd finished eating and I was beginning to think he's not too bad really when Teri Hatcher came straight off the set of Desperate Housewives and turned up wanting to know if he was missing her and why hadn't he returned her calls!'

'Oh dear. Sorry Chloe. That's a bit tough. What did he say to this woman?'

'He said he was sorry but it wasn't convenient right now as he was entertaining his neighbour. At which point she screamed, 'You two-timing bastard,' slapped him and stormed off.'

Davina stifled a giggle and I found myself wanting to laugh too so we both let go.

But Davina was desperate to salvage the situation. 'But did he have any kind of explanation for you?'

'He turned into a bungling idiot and spluttered his way through this pathetic apology about how he'd meant to tell Miranda that it was all over between them but hadn't got round to it. He said he was very keen to get to know *me* now! Marvellous, hey!'

'Ah. Rotten news darling. More P.F. required.'

It got to the point when I knew that I'd definitely had too much to drink and to go home would be a sensible idea.

'Davina, I think it's time to..' But just then Andrew walked in with Chantal and I had one of those ridiculous moments when I decided that staying was a better idea.

'Andrew! Chantal! You really must come and join us. We're having quite a party over here.' There weren't enough seats for them so I attempted a standing position but stumbled in my high heels and giggled.

'Oh, thanks Chloe but we're only staying for one. You see we have a table booked at Nobu.' I hated the way he looked so gorgeous as he rejected me. So he was taking two-planks Chantal to Nobu. She probably wouldn't even understand the menu. Davina then came to my rescue, threw an arm round me and said,

'Now you mention it we're off to dinner as well. See you Monday!'

And with that I was pushed out of the door and forced to face the fresh air. I can't remember much more.

When I woke up this morning it was a good job I had a hangover. A clear head would have allowed me to wonder what the hell there was to look forward to and right now that would be a slippery slope to despair. And then, as if by magic, Davina appeared at my bedroom door.

'I've made you a cup of tea, darling.' She said quietly and placed it gently on the bedside table. I looked at the clock.

'Don't worry, it's Saturday.'

Somehow that seemed small comfort.

'Listen, I'll stick around today. I'll squeeze into a pair of your jeans and you can show me the delights of Hartfield and we could even do a bit of retail therapy. What do you say?'

'Wonderful.' I managed and even though it sounded as if I wasn't grateful, I was.

Becky

I was just pulling up this bloody great thistle when there was an enormous crash in the house. I looked round but I couldn't see Jack. He'd been there. Just a second before. I rushed into the house and there he was staring down at his toys, scattered over the floor along with the shelf and everything else that I'd put on it.

I picked him up and held him tight. He seemed OK. Probably thought it was some sort of game. Watch Mummy put up a shelf and a few weeks later watch it fall down again. I was only trying to make the place seem a bit tidier. There was stuff everywhere but the only thing I really noticed was the pot plant that Mrs Robinson gave me and how the soil was everywhere.

But then I burst into tears. You see I just didn't know what to do. Then I remembered what Mrs Robinson had said about not being too proud to ask for help when things get tough. So I found myself, still holding Jack of course, knocking on the neighbour's door like some sort of desperate woman. There was no answer at first, so I knocked louder and I was about to start screaming when Alex finally showed his face.

'Ah, hello. Er, Becky. Yes. Hello Becky.' He said and I wondered if he was all there, you know what I mean, but I decided I'd better be polite anyway. He looked at Jack like the little love might bite him.

'And you must be..'

'It's Jack actually.' I reminded him.

'Ah, yes. Jack. Good day to you sir.'

Strange thing to say to a two year old boy, but never mind Jack seemed to like it and he even smiled.

'Alex, I'm really sorry to have to ask you but you see the shelf in the lounge has fallen down and all the stuff's just everywhere and I just don't know what to do. Can you help me?'

'Right.'

He says the oddest things this bloke. What's right about it? Then he didn't say anthin' for ages. Just scratched his head before saying it again.

'Right.' It was a bit more like he meant it this time and so I thought maybe we're gettin' somewhere.

'Just give me a minute and I'll be right there.'

He disappeared and I didn't really know what to do so I just stood there outside his door, holding Jack. It seemed like ages before he came back.

'Right, shall we go?'

I expected him to turn up with a tool box or maybe even a change of clothes after all the time he'd been but, no, he was exactly as before, not a screwdriver in sight. He's a mystery to me this man. But still he was coming to help.

I suddenly felt quite embarrassed as we both stared down at my pathetic belongings but then Alex picked up the pot plant that Mrs Robinson had given me and sort of put it back together. He didn't say a word and I wondered for a minute if he thought I wanted a hand with the tidying up. Then he started knocking on the wall, where the screws had been and then in other places. Finally he actually said something.

'Won't be a minute.' And with that he was gone.

I couldn't help imagining him running straight past his door, to the end of the lane and taking for the hills never to be seen again. I could just see the front page of the local paper; 'Alex Minty-Kempton sees Becky Wright's fallen shelf and scarpers!'

But no, just a few minutes later and he's back this time holding a posh shiny tool box in one hand and an electric drill in the other. Things were looking up.

'Cup of tea?' I offered.

'Thank you Becky that would be lovely.' And all of a sudden I thought we're goin' to get along just peachy, so I offered him a biscuit as well.

Jack just sat on the floor and stared at Alex going about his work. I wasn't sure if it was the chocolate biscuit that was transformin' him or that Mummy finally had a man in the house doing something for her. Pity it was just fixing a shelf, eh?

'Now Becky, let me show you something.'

He showed me these special screws with special raw plugs that open up and then he tapped on the wall again.

'You see Becky, this is a partition wall so it's not very thick so you either use these,' he put them in my hand, 'or you would need to put the shelf up on this other wall.'

It all sounded too technical for me.

'What so I've gotta have me shelf on that wall or use these special screws?'

'That's exactly it.'

'What do ya think's best mate? Cos there, it's over the sofa and I wouldn't want it crashing on me head, especially little Jack's.'

'Mm. Well it wouldn't crash, not with the right fittings but equally we could put it up again on the same wall so that this time it was secure.'

Suddenly I was beginning to like this man a lot. I liked that he said *we* could put it up when it's pretty bloody obvious it's going be him. I sort of knew I wanted it back where it was, but all safe of course, but most of all I trusted him so somehow it didn't matter.

'Can I 'ave it back where it was? That would suit me best.'

'Of course you can Becky.' And with that he set to work.

I decided to take Jack out into the garden to keep out of his way and that's where Alex found us when he'd finished.

He stood at the back door and looked all around at everything. The Magnolia tree which has the most amazing purple flowers at this time and then all the bulbs in the pots and the…. It was as if he was memorised and he didn't say nothin' for ages. But then he said.

'Becky, this is magnificent!'

Wow! I thought. No one's ever said anything about me that's magnificent before.

'Thanks ever so. We do our best, me and little Jack.'

'Well your best is quite something. You've obviously got green fingers.'

'You see I learnt a bit from Mrs Robinson. She's 82 and she's got a massive garden which is just amazin'. I used to clean for her.' I wished I hadn't said that last bit.

'Has Mrs Robinson seen this garden?'

'Nah, she's never been over here. You see neither of us have a car and what with her being so old it's easier for me to get the bus over to her's.'

'Right.' He said and this time I could tell he was thinkin' stuff but not saying it.

'Well, I'd better be off.' He said and you know I was quite sad he was going.

That evening I had a smile on my face and I kept repeating the word magnificent in my mind and sometimes out loud. Jack just stared at me. I think he thought it was a game. Magnificent! Magnificent! Magnificent!

Alex

I used to buy the pink pages every day. It was part of the job and even AR (After Redundancy) I continued with the daily ritual. After all, I needed to be up to date with financial affairs just in case another chance at City life was on offer. Then the other week, when I was busy with the house move, I sort of made a conscious (or was it subconscious) decision to stop. It sort of marked my resignation to the fact that I won't be going back. And you know, just recently, plan B is looking increasingly attractive and I have a feeling, not for any particular reason you understand, but just a feeling that it's getting closer.

However, I still get the Saturday FT. It seems safe with its light-hearted weekend editorial wrapping the investment news. But I look at it in a different light now. 'How to Spend It', the magazine supplement, used to be a chance to decide what luxury item I would buy that weekend. Something impressive either due to the designer label before its functional name or for its sheer extravagance. And, of course, I would slip into conversation with friends and colleagues,

'Seen the latest MP3 Player that fits into your trainers so you can measure your fitness levels whilst listening to Mahler? Well, I happen to lay my hands on one at the weekend. Seems pretty good.'

Now I look at these objects of desire and look at the price and think about what else that sort of money could buy. This morning I decided that for the price of the latest Sat Nav I could have 10 bottles of decent Bordeaux or 25 take-aways or get new leather seats for the Bentley.

There's more than meets the eye to Becky at number three. She came knocking on my door the other day. Actually banging it down in hysteria would be closer to the truth. I don't know what it is about the women in this lane. Anyway, I don't mind telling you that I was a bit taken aback at first. Mainly by her manner. But I thought about it, how she brings that child up on her own with little money and how she would need a bit of help from time to time. All she wanted was a shelf re-fixing so that it was safe. Didn't take long as I have the tools for the job. Funny, how the first time I use that tool box is for one of the neighbours. Mother bought it for me as a moving- in present. Just goes to show there's not a lot of DIY going on here. Made me think about this place. But the remarkable thing was her garden. You come out of the back of this simple little cottage with no surprises to find an oasis of calm and beauty. I don't mind telling you I was impressed by what she's done with her little piece of England. Got me thinking about my own garden. There's not much to it really. Bit of an old patio, a patchy lawn and a few shrubs that look like they've seen better days. Not very appealing at all. Next thing I know I'm in a garden centre looking at decking and lawn feed and a few flowers.

Funny thing was, Becky caught me unloading the Bentley when I got home.

'Alex! Hi there! Been to the garden centre? Need a hand unloading?'

'Oh, Hello Becky. Yes, you've motivated me to do something with my patch at the back. Not a spot on yours, of course.'

'Oh, well, if you need a hand.'

And I thought I could do with a bit of advice, so why not.

'Thanks, I'd like that.'

Her face lit up as if helping me out would be an absolute pleasure to her.

I made tea and we sat on a couple of old deck chairs perusing the turgid landscape. Jack enjoyed the space the lawn gave him to run around. I thought it would turn me into a nervous wreck having a two year old on my property but he seemed harmless enough.

'So what you got planned?' Becky asked me.

'Bit of an impulse buy actually. Not much planning has gone on so far. I just felt inspired by what you've achieved next door.'

'Ah bless. You say ever so nice things. But actually it wasn't too bad when I moved in a year ago so I've just added bits and kept it all going.'

'Did Mrs Robinson help you?'

'Well yes. She was my intervening, like you say. She gave me cuttings from her place and told me sunshine or shade, clay or lime, wet or dry. All the little plants needs and wants and I just followed that. But sometimes I think just givin' them a bit of attention is what makes them grow.'

'I think you've just defined "green fingers".'

'I don't know about that but I do know I'm proud of it.'

As she said that she picked Jack up to play with him and I thought it must be damned hard being a single parent. Eventually she sat down and said,

'What are we like! I've got the answer to all this. I'll do a load of cuttings from my garden and you can put them in here and soon you'll be well away!'

'Oh, Becky, that would be marvellous.'

'Marvellous!' she said mocking my accent but I didn't mind and we had a jolly good laugh together.
Uncomplicated. That's how I'd describe Becky. It's a shame Chloe isn't the same in that respect. I know I'm not the perfect catch but I just have a feeling we'd be good together. I got a take-away the other evening, one from the better Indian restaurant in the village, opened a decent drop of vino and knocked on her door. I thought she was going to turn me down at first. She looked quite taken aback and a bit tired if I'm honest but then luckily she came to her senses. She wanted time to get ready, so I thought, Alex, it's your lucky night!

We got on really well. Talked about all sorts and I even

put her in the picture about working up in the City. She didn't seem fazed and she didn't turn on the sympathy which I was pleased about.

Then, just as I was about to move things along, bloody Miranda turns up! Couldn't believe it; What rotten luck! And all down to the timing. I mean if I'd got round to cooling it off with Miranda, which I had every intention of doing, she simply wouldn't have come round on spec like that. In fact I expect the reason she did was because I've been avoiding her. You know, letting her down gently by not returning her calls for a few days.

So the evening ends in disaster. Miranda goes crazy and hits me and Chloe, not in the least bit convinced by my honest explanation, storms off!

Question is, what do I do now? I got up early this morning, threw on a dressing gown and casually opened my front door as Chloe was leaving her house. I waved and smiled with a civil 'Good Morning!' and she practically scowled at me.

It seems as though her divorce has left her scarred which must be awful for her but all the more reason to move on, put it behind her and start seeing someone else. I know we could have some fun together. I suppose a take-away is a bit pedestrian to a high flyer like Chloe. I need to take her somewhere romantic. I know, Hever Castle! Yes, the Italian gardens there are quite spectacular. Erotic even! Perfect! I had a leaflet through the door the other day about the Lakeside Theatre there. Just need to decide whether a spot of Shakespeare or a bit of light opera will be her scene. She'll be so impressed; it's bound to soften her up. After all, I've never taken Miranda anywhere like that.

I cancelled the order for the decking. When I was in the garden centre I thought it would look great and cover up some of the weeds. I didn't want to transport it in the Bentley so I asked for it to be delivered. But now I think about it, Becky doesn't have any decking at all. And it cost quite a bit, so I think I'll spend the money on plants instead. I'll give the patio a good clean, dig over the beds for new planting and give the lawn a bit of tender loving care to start off with. And what with Becky's kind offer of help, well, it will take time but I'm sure the end result will be worth waiting for.

Sheila

I still haven't booked the holiday. It's gone from being a small thing that I'll get round to, to this humungous thing that I can't even bear to think about. I even crossed the road today when I saw the travel agents just two doors down. George hasn't asked so far, but I know he will. So I'm avoiding him too. It's getting ridiculous. I got home from choir the other day and I was stood outside my own front door with the key poised in my hand but somehow I just couldn't bring myself to go in. It was like I was frozen in time. I don't know how long I stayed like that but I felt this gentle tap on my shoulder and when I looked round it was Chloe.

'Everything OK, Sheila?' she said gently. She's very nice, Chloe, and I didn't see much point in putting up some sort of pretence in front of her. Somehow, I knew she'd understand.

'No, I don't think I am.'

She smiled at me and didn't seem shocked at all. She didn't laugh nervously not knowing whether I was joking or not; she just put an arm around me and said,

'Would you like to come into mine for a cup of tea?'

'Yes, I'd like that,' I said knowing that at least it would put off the inevitable.

Chloe's house is lovely and very peaceful. It's all warm colours and cosy sofas. Living on her own, I suppose she can have it anyway she wants.

'How do you take your tea?'

'Just normal. Just milk.' I replied and wondered if that was boring and almost wished I had it black with a slice of lemon.

'Do sit down; make yourself comfortable,' she said and I sank into the softness of this big red sofa. It felt wonderful, like someone was cuddling me. I picked up a big plump cushion and hugged it. Chloe came back in and pulled up a little table to put the tea on so that it was right in front of me.

'Thanks Chloe.'

'Anytime.'

She sat opposite me and didn't say anything for ages. Just sipped her tea and smiled occasionally.

'Everything alright with you?' I asked.

'Pretty awful,' she said but not in a way which made you think that it was that bad really.

'Oh, I'm sorry to hear that.'

'Don't worry. I'll get over it. It's just things going wrong at work and ... other stuff as well.'

'Right.' I didn't really know what to say but I came out with, 'I'm sure it will all work out in the end.' It sounded like something George would say so I added, 'well either that, or it will get you down and you'll go crazy one day.'

She laughed and I joined in and it felt nice.

'I've already gone crazy, darling,' she said. Now, enough about me. Do you want to tell me what's so awful about the other side of your front door?'

And then I realised she must have seen me standing there for some time. I realised it was the fact that I had to face George who doesn't know about my double life.

'I haven't booked the holiday for this year, yet. Not that's it always down to me but normally we're booked by now and George raised it the other day so I said I'd do it, but I haven't.'

She smiled but said nothing.

'But really it's David.'

'David?'

'My son. He doesn't come over very often.'

'Oh, I see.' She said but of course she didn't see and I decided more than anything I wanted to tell her.

'David's gay.'

'Right,' she said, as if I'd just said it's raining.

'It's not a problem for me. It's just the way he is. But it's George. Ever since David told us, George doesn't even really want to see his son. I invite him round for Sunday lunch every now and then but George stays silent through the meal and then goes straight back into the shed. He just can't come to terms with it. When Wendy, our daughter comes and brings our granddaughter he couldn't be more pleased. But with David well...'

'That must be very difficult to cope with.' You see I knew she'd understand.

'I've been coping with it for years now but the other evening.. well, it all suddenly got more complicated.'

'What happened?' Chloe asked and I was pleased she'd asked because I didn't want to ramble on boring her with my problems if she wasn't interested.

'I spoke to David on the telephone and he told me he's moving back to Hartfield. He's bought The Green Antiques shop and the flat above.'

'That's wonderful.' Chloe said and for a moment it was *just* wonderful. Perhaps because she could see it too. How I would be able to see my son so much more.

'I haven't told George yet. Oh, and he's bringing his partner, Nigel, with him.' I added, as if this was just a minor detail when in fact the very thought has been keeping me awake at night.

'More tea?' Chloe offered. I thought of George wanting his dinner at the usual time.

'Yes, please.' He'll have to wait.

Not until milk and tea were poured and stirred and we'd both sat back in our comfy sofas did Chloe speak.

'Well, David's moving back whatever. It's just a case of when and how George finds out. Perhaps you should let the grand scheme of things take its course.' She took a sip of her tea and then added, 'after all it sounds like it's George with the problem here.'

I could have hugged her. It felt like suddenly I could fling open doors and find nothing but joy.

'You're right, it's George's problem.' And with that said out loud it felt OK to dream of what might be.

'It seems quite wonderful that David will be living down the road in just a couple of weeks. I talked to him about maybe helping out in the shop and he said "what a good idea, I'll pay you, of course." I don't want to be paid. Just to be a part of his life is enough.'

Chloe smiled. 'It's such a lovely shop. You might even learn a bit about antiques! Think of the possibilities!'

I like that word. Possibilities. It's full of hope and exciting things to come. I don't even know what they are, but just the fact that possibilities are out there and they must be because Chloe said so and she's very bright. My tea was drunk and the bottom of the cup was no longer scary.

'I'd better go and put George's dinner on. He likes it at six-thirty normally.' Chloe's clock said ten past seven but the hands seemed to gently rest on the roman numerals and it seemed OK. As I got up to go I realised that I'd learnt very little about Chloe except that she made me feel better.

'Pop round for a cup of tea, any time,' I said and she smiled.

'I will.'

George

Amy, she's my granddaughter, was absolutely thrilled with the doll's house. Her mother was really impressed too.

'Dad, I can't believe you've made it,' she said. 'It's wonderful. Thank you. What do you say Amy?'

Seeing the little girl's face light up is all I need. I'd driven over there specially one Thursday afternoon. I mentioned it to Sheila but she said she was busy with the choir so I thought I'll go on my own.

'It must have taken you ages.'

'Well I have a lot of time on my hands since I've left the force.'

'I bet Mum's glad the mess is all cleared away now.'

'Actually I made it in the shed. Shelia doesn't really come in.'

'Is it good for you Dad; spending all that time out there?'

'I'm happy in my shed,' I said and didn't feel the need to elaborate. I mean I don't expect Wendy to understand any more than Sheila does.

'How's Mum?'

'Well she's better now I think, but she's still not really herself.'

'So she's not on the tablets anymore?'

'No, they're finished with.'

'Well that's good.'

Mrs Johnson in the travel agents looks like she couldn't get up from her desk if she tried. Of course the first thing I asked her was if Sheila had been in, just in case she'd already booked.

'No, your wife hasn't been in; I expect she's been busy.'

'She's busy alright,' I couldn't help saying but shouldn't have really.

'I'm looking for Cornwall, self catering, a cottage for four adults and two children.'

'Oh, you're going with family this year?'

'Yes, my daughter Wendy and her family; little Amy is only four.'

'I'm sure you'll have a lovely time,' she said reaching for her glasses and peering at her screen. There was a long pause that I felt the need to fill.

'We went last year. St Ives. Had a good time, although it did rain.'

'You definitely want self catering? There are some good hotel deals in September?'

'I think Sheila would prefer to do most of the cooking.'

'OK then.' She looked doubtful but with Wendy to help out I think it's the best solution. After all children are fussy eaters at the best of times.

'There's not a lot at the beginning of September; you're booking rather late.'

'I know. I said to Sheila we need to get going but she said leave it to me and now she's done nothing. But still she's not been well.'

'Oh, I'm sorry to hear that. Nothing serious I hope?'

'No, no, nothing serious.'

I'd spoken to Wendy on the phone and she said that would be lovely but it would be a case of when they could fit it in.

'Well, we'll fit round you; after all now I'm retired we can go anytime.'

'Right well I'll discuss it with Andy this evening.'

I felt disappointed even though I shouldn't have.

'I'll call you tomorrow though,' she said which is fair enough. When she called she said they could only do the first week in September.

'Ah, this looks right.' Mrs Johnson bounced in her chair but didn't get very far as she was wedged in. 'It's a lovely scenic place called 'Over the Edge', right on the coast at Tintagel and has the sort of thing you're looking for.' She looked at me as if she wanted a yes or no answer there and then.

'Right, so tell me more.'

'Three bedrooms, lovely sea views, cliff top situation.'

'What about the children? It doesn't sound suitable for a four year old.'

Mrs Johnson sighed. 'Right well we'll keep looking for you. It's just that you've left it rather late.' She looked rather serious for a while until finally she said, 'Center Parcs. Have you ever considered that?'

They look nice on the telly but my friend Johnny said they're a bit pricey.

'How much?' I asked.

She read out a few details and gave me different prices for different options.

'Is that in Cornwall?'

'No, Longleat, Wiltshire.'

'I thought you were looking in Cornwall?'

'You know it doesn't matter what the weather's like when you go to Center Parcs. There's lots of activities for young and old. It's very popular with families.'

It's at times like these I'm just glad I've got the shed; somewhere away from all the complexities of life. Anyway I told her to hold the Center Parcs option for me and I'd discuss it with Sheila and be back to book the next day. I daren't go ahead there and then.

So I was sat at home waiting for her to arrive. Six thirty came and went. We normally eat at that time. Finally she turned up at 7.15. Looked a bit sheepish but I decided best not to say anything.

'Alright dear?'

'Yes, everything's fine.'

'Shall I pop up the road and get fish and chips, save you cooking?'

'Good idea,' she said.

She didn't even warm the plates and insist on serving them at the table. We sat on the sofa and ate them out of the paper. After we'd finished I made us both a cup of tea and then I broached the subject. I had a brochure the travel agent had given me and opened it at the right page. Sheila had a good look.

'So Wendy's definitely coming?' she asked.

'Yes, as long as we book that week.'

'It says here it doesn't matter what the weather is like there's still lots to do. I see there's a spa.'

'Yes, you'll enjoy that won't you?'

And she actually smiled.

'No sheds though,' she said.

'I'll manage.'

Chloe

Work was becoming a major source of stress. Nourriture Verte's share price was defiantly falling despite all my efforts and the whole situation became one I dreaded. Robin's attitude didn't help.

'Just what are you doing about it, Chloe?' I was sat in his office feeling like a naughty school girl as he turned his pen from end to end and stared at it as if he couldn't bear to look at me.

'The whole Euro desk has suffered a dip but Nourriture Verte is heading for disaster.'

The blame culture F&C adopted, topped with Robin's hands-off-if-anything-goes-wrong- it-is-your-fault style of management, was enough to make you go home and bake cakes. He continued his rant.

'Lord Barrington rang me this morning. Apparently Lady Barrington has invested some of her portfolio in Green, including N.V.. They are not best pleased. I think we should cut our losses. Sell and put the proceeds into something safe. Then move it back if N.V. recovers. What do you think?'

This was seriously underhand and, of course, something safe would not be a Green stock.

'But what do we tell investors?'

'I don't know, make something up!'

Now, I was desperate. 'Give me a few weeks to work on N.V. Then we'll make a decision.'

'You're pushing me Chloe!'

He got up and paced the room. Then it was back to his chair and his pen, tap, tap, bloody tap.

'Okay, but it better be good.'

'Thanks Robin,' although I said it quietly I had to wonder why I was thanking him at all?

As I left his office he shouted, 'I hear you can get cheap flights to Tours from Stansted.'

Marvellous, I thought. The problem, of course, was Éduardo Devereux, the CEO of Nourriture Verte. I could never get a satisfactory response from him by e-mail and getting hold of him on the phone was impossible. So, when you actually got through, it was a bit of a shock and even though I read out my prepared script beautifully he simply became charm personified, emulating reassurance and positive outcomes.

The cheap flight at inhumane o'clock from Stansted, which is an hour further away from Lodge Lane than my usual Gatwick, left me less than fighting fit although probably angry enough to pack a punch. But the sight of N.V.'s headquarters, nestling in the hills of the Loire Valley with the sun shining over it lifted me. The taxi dropped me at reception.

The building was actually a converted farmhouse, beautifully quaint from the outside and yet they have modernised the inside to give it an air of professionalism. The boardroom itself is a converted barn with large sheets of glass providing idyllic views over the farmlands of this thriving (I pray) enterprise. I had a peep in the small kitchen just off the main room and noticed it was stocked with all the business's own brands, with a packet of English tea looking awkward amongst them. I was handed a cup of water that must have boiled earlier that day and a tea bag to do its worst.

Éduardo entered the room and I wondered if he thought being dashingly handsome and exquisitely dressed was an important part of his job. I had met him before, once, but somehow he was having more impact this time. Maybe it was the waft of aftershave or the way he smiled at me for an uncomfortably long time.

'Bonjour Chloe. It is such a pleasure to have your company.' He scanned the room and forced a range of thin smiles across the vast board room table. As he linked his lap top to the projector he said,

'I have a presentation for you!' in the same why you might tell a lover that you've just booked a romantic weekend in Paris. I had a list of questions I was keen to put to them and some suggestions to make having done my own research. This presentation, I suspected, would be underwhelming and time wasting. I opened my briefcase to retrieve my notes and then realised that Davina had planted a roll of duct tape; her way of reminding me to carefully select the time to speak out and the time to deploy patience. I allowed a small smile, but nothing more, towards Éduardo in acceptance of his offering.

By the fifth slide I was bored with what I already knew: how they had set up the company, what their plans were, why there is a growing demand for organic produce. The falling share price got a mention and was described as unexpected and just a blip in their fortunes. There were new ideas, diversification, and future projects but all lacked substance and the financial forecast and research to back them up. I looked round the room. Ten of them; one of me. Why wasn't Robin here to help me? Finally Eduardo sat down. They all looked at me expectantly. It was time to remove the duct tape and swallow a diplomacy pill.

'Thank you,' I began. 'I've listened with interest.' Well they wouldn't let me interrupt anyway. 'I'm particularly keen to know more detail on your diversification plans. Having done my own research,' papers were shuffled nervously around the room, 'I would think that some of these projects would require considerable investment. Do you have the capital ready?'

Alain Boutard, their financial director, spluttered on his water.

'What is the expected ROI of each?' I continued. Eduardo turned to Alain, 'A question for you, I think.'
Alain looked for a sheet of paper in front of him and didn't find it.

'The fact is that these projects are in the early stages of development and we do not have the full financial forecast yet,' he said hopefully.

'But you do have the capital investment?' It just fell out in frustration.

'Not exactly. Well not for all of it,' he squirmed.

'How much?' I could see Davina poised with the duct tape.

'A modest figure, but we expect the rest to come from future growth in revenue.'

'But surely you will need that for your shareholders?'

Eduardo chimed in, 'the shareholders must understand that this is a long-term investment. We are talking, 3, 5 years before the real returns come to them.' I was desperate, I had two weeks. 'But I have shareholders *now*, wanting to see a turnaround in the share price.'

'Yes, and we must do everything we can to help you, Chloe. And we will!' Despite their excellent English there was a language barrier or perhaps a stubbornness on their side to understand but the fight was out of me. I played my last card softly, 'Eduardo, I have to inform you that if there is not significant and hard evidence of a turnaround in the next two weeks it may be F&C's decision to sell our shareholding.' There I'd said it. At least it felt better blaming Robin. After all, *I* would stick with it.

'I see,' he looked concerned, not angry, and said gently but with sincerity, 'We value your time, Chloe, the fact that you have come here today, and your honesty and we understand your situation. I will do everything I can to make F&C change their mind. I hope it's enough.' The delivery was more moving than the words. Perhaps the message had got through. As we finished off the formalities I couldn't help warming to this man. I thought as I left, that maybe the duct tape should have gone over my eyes.

My hosts had checked me into a charming guesthouse down in the village so much better than the large, soulless hotels I was used to. As if on auto pilot I opened up my lap top and realised that a wireless connection was unlikely but a few clicks proved me wrong. The emails could only serve to spoil my day but curiosity is always a big a draw for me. My eyes scanned the senders and I decided I would pick out and read from friend but not foe.

Sender: Davina
Subject: Duct tape

Darling, always remember, the French are a sensitive bunch. Charm them with your good looks and keep this little reminder in front of you at all times!
Hugs, Davina x

The next email was more than surprising. How had my neighbour, Alex, got hold of my email address? Then I realised, it was quite easy to work out with a quick visit to the F&C website. And of course he knows that I work there.

Sender: Alex
Subject: Apologies

Dear Chloe, Just wanted to apologise for the mishap the other evening. All a dreadful misunderstanding which I'm sure you've realised by now. I will admit Miranda has been a friend of mine for some time but really there is no romance any longer. So you see, there was no need for you to storm off like that.

Enjoyed your company immensely over the take-away and it was so lovely to have a proper conversation with you at last.

Would love to rectify the situation with an outing to Hever Castle and tickets for the Lakeside theatre. There's Shakespeare's 'Much Ado About Nothing' or Noel Coward's 'Present Laughter' on offer. Any thoughts?

Looking out on to Lodge Lane I see your charming Mini Cooper is not around.
Be safe
Best regards
Alex

The audacity of this man is quite astonishing and yet I had to laugh at his scheme to 'rectify the situation'. I don't think I've ever met a man who can endear himself to me at the same time as making my blood boil! I hit the reply button, spotted the duct tape and pressed escape.

Just then the telephone rang and startled I began to think that Alex must know where I am!

'Allo?'

'Chloe! C'est Éduardo, Bonsoir! I was just wondering if you would like to join me for dinner? I know a wonderful Peu de bistro where we could go.'

What was it about audacious men? I seem to attract them! How could we flick the switch from drawing battle lines to amiable company. Hearing my silence he continued,

'I realise the meeting was difficult and I want to ensure you have a pleasant evening. You must be hungry, yes? I'm sure glass of wine and some French cuisine will help you to relax after today.' Well, he was right about that.

'I suppose I do need to eat.' The fact was (who was I kidding?) I was tired and frustrated enough to be reckless.

'Excellent, I am waiting for you in your hotel reception.'

'You're here in my hotel?'

'Yes, I apologise, I took the liberty of coming in. I so hoped you would have dinner with me.'

I looked at myself in the mirror. I looked tired in my suit and desperately wanted to shower and change. He read my silence again.

'Please take your time. You may want to freshen up. I'm happy to wait.'

'One question, this bistro; is it informal; can I wear jeans?'

'Of course, Chloe, casual is perfect.'

With a quick shower and tomorrow's blouse over a pair of jeans I felt much more human despite the fact that I had been up for 15 hours already. The taxi seemed to climb the mountainside for miles and whilst we chatted easily by the time we got to this out of the way restaurant on the edge of a remote village I was convinced he must be married. But then this was always going to be an irresponsible evening.

Our table was nestled in an alcove and once seated I found myself delighting in his conversation. He was well versed in politics, different cultures, you name it, and had either been fully briefed on London life the previous day or had a strong interest in the City. I found myself laughing again and again and the time slipped away. All too soon the taxi returned us to my hotel. I knew this was ill-fated but at least it provided a delicious diversion. So when he stepped out of the cab with me and paid the driver to leave us alone the decision to invite him to my bed to conclude this brief encounter was an easy one.

Lodge Lane was grey with rain and as I shut the front door I noticed the answer machine flashing and the post splayed on the door mat but both could wait. Armed with a decent cup of tea and a bar of chocolate straight from the fridge I found myself staring through the kitchen window at my own garden. There was something different about it; all the plants a little perkier, the lawn greener and the weeds gone; surely it wasn't just the rain. I thought of Jenny, my cleaner, but only momentarily as I often wonder if she even does the two hours that I pay her to clean the house. Then I thought of Becky, who I know is keen on gardening but she's also terribly shy. Sheila's way too occupied with her own problems. Which left Alex, and which reminded me, his email is still sitting in my inbox. Despite the fact that, right at that moment, I'd rather go to bed and sleep for an indulgent twelve hours, I extracted my lap top from my luggage, fired it up, found the offending email and hit reply.

Alex

Becky came round the other day to help me with my garden. She knocked on my door, bold as brass, and said,
'Alex, you gardenin', today?'
Must admit, I was only on my first espresso and a general plan for the day was yet to form but as the sun was shining, I replied 'Splendid idea Becky. Just give me ten minutes and I'll be right with you.'
'I'll let me self in round the back then and get started.' And with that she was gone.

We had made good progress by lunch time with some of the beds dug over, and a feed applied to the lawn. Wanting to thank Becky in some small way I suggested a French style lunch of bread and cheese. She looked at me quizzically.
'Sounds dead posh that. Me and little Jack, we have sarnies if we're lucky.' She was laughing as she said it. Still she tucked in and said how lovely it all was so I was pleased.
'It's very good of you to help me, Becky.'
'Well it's a good opportunity with Jack at playgroup. It's funny but it's not like work at all. I really love it; gettin' out here and gettin' amongst it.'
'Been in touch with Mrs Robinson recently?' I asked
'Nah, not for a couple of weeks. I worry sometimes, the age she is. She won't 'ave no mobile phone 'cos she's 82 and it would be too much for her but if she did I could text; make sure every now and then.'
'I'd like to meet this Mrs Robinson.'
'What you?! What really?! Whatever for?!'
'Well for a start off I'd love to see her garden. Any woman over 82 who can keep things going gains my admiration. Yes, I think you and I should pay her a visit.'

'Cor blimey Alex. You're not short of a few surprises! Well I think that would be mega but you up to goin' on the bus?'

'I was going to suggest that we go in the Bentley actually. What do you think?'

'I think that's bleedin' splendid!' Again she mocked my accent and we both laughed as we relaxed back into our chairs to let our lunch digest and enjoy the satisfaction brought about by seeing the garden coming along nicely.

So yesterday, with young Jack being looked after by Sheila, we set off. I couldn't help noticing that Becky had put on a bit of make-up and she was wearing freshly ironed jeans and a T-shirt. As she climbed into the Bentley beside me she was grinning like a child off to the fairground. She struggled with the seat belt,

'Gently does it,' I advised.

'Gently is bleedin' useless! This thing needs a good yank.'

Amazingly the seat belt remained intact.

'So, are you navigating, Becky?'

'Ah no! I don't know nothin' about navigating.'

'OK, where does Mrs Robinson reside?'

'I don't know nothin' about that either but I usually get the bus to Halstead.'

'Splendid! Halstead, here we come!'

As I started up the engine Becky looked concerned. 'This thing safe is it?'

'Becky, my dear, I wouldn't take you out in it if it wasn't safe.' That seemed to put her mind at rest. She rolled down the window and leant her arm out. I could only assume she was day dreaming after that. She had a big smile on her face and she didn't say a word until we reached Mrs Robinson's village.

'See there, that big white house with the wisteria all over it, that's the one.'

I pulled on to the gravel driveway and thought what a beautiful little spot. Becky jumped out of the car.

'I'd better warn her first. You know, tell her I've got me mate with me today.'

It's funny but Mrs Robinson was everything I'd imagined from her silver hair knotted in a bun to her petite stature with her spine gently curved with age. I decided it was safe to approach and as I did Becky explained, 'So 'ere he is, Mrs Robinson, you see he's alright when you get to know him.'

'Alex Minter-Kemp.' I offered my hand.

'Edie Robinson. Pleasure to meet you. And thank you so much for bringing Becky. This is a treat!'

Then followed the grand tour of the garden. It must have taken close to half an hour although the time flew by. Edie knew all her plants intricately and recounted their stories including both the good times and the bad and I had to smile as Becky chipped in every now and then;

'I planted that.'

'I pruned that one.'

'I weeded this section.'

Edie smiled too and by the time we were back at the house I'd really warmed to the little lady. She was soon sitting at the garden table as if she needed a rest and Becky went inside to make the tea.

'The biscuits are in the usual place,' Edie called out to her as she went through the French windows.

'Right you are Mrs R.'

Edie then turned to me and smiled before she said. 'So Alex, what brings you to these parts?'

And for the first time since the dreaded redundancy I was completely straight about all that has gone on over the last year. No vagueness, no dressing up the truth and no talk of going back to the City but just the cold reality, although somehow it didn't seem so cold anymore. Somehow, Mrs R provided a safe pair of ears. I even found myself telling her how much I like living in Lodge Lane.

'It's a splendid little spot actually, right in the centre of a charming village. Everything going for it; even got nice neighbours!'

'You have certainly struck lucky with Becky!' Edie said and I smiled.

'The cottage is smaller than I'm used to, but it means I don't have a mortgage, so as long as I get some form of work soon, I shall be alright.'

It was great because she just sat and listened patiently; didn't interrupt me. And as I spoke, the funny thing was, it was all as much a realisation for me that I've reached this point, as it was for her. When I got to the end she simply said,

'It's good to hear you're settling in so well.'

Becky turned up with the tea and having served everyone she sat down and said,

'See he's alright really, Mrs Robinson. Don't you think?' Even though he talks funny he's not a bad bloke. He put a shelf up for me, you know? One that had fallen down, that is.'

Edie grinned, 'Did he really, Becky, well that's very kind!' She sat back and then turned to me. 'Do you have a garden, Alex?'

'Yes, I do. Nothing like the size of this one but I'm very fortunate to have Becky to help me get it into shape.'

'Ah,' she responded and then there was a very long pause until she said, 'so you're *both* gardeners.'

'Oh, I don't know much about it really,' I had to confess. 'Becky's the brains behind it. I'm just learning as I go along.'

'Nothing wrong with that,' Edie said.

The next time I looked over she'd put her head back and was snoozing in the sunshine.

'She does that,' Becky explained. 'It's 'cos she's 82. At that age you just go off, just like that, no word of warnin'. She'll be back with us shortly.'

'Good to hear it.'

When she did emerge from her nap it was as if the last ten minutes hadn't happened and she simply said,

'You two should go into business together. The gardening business. And I will be your first client.'

Becky and I looked at each other and I sensed she was quite uncomfortable about the idea. I must admit it struck me as being pretty crazy although there was something about it that fitted my ideas around plan B beautifully. For a moment there Becky seemed lost for words, not something you experience often but then she made her own sense of it.

'Mrs Robinson, if you need any help you've only got to ask. You don't need to become no client.'

'That's very kind Becky but the very fact is that I've been thinking of employing some help for a while now. It's getting too much for me really. I just want to be able to potter. Anyway, the point is I'd much rather pay you than some stranger.'

'Well that's one thing but I don't know nothin' about no business now do I?'

'Ah, but you see that's where Alex comes in. I'm sure he could work out how to set up a small business. What do you say Alex?'

When we got back to Lodge Lane I noticed Chloe's car was back and decided I'd check my emails. Sure enough there was a reply from the lady herself.

Subject: Apologies

Dear Alex,
Apology accepted – after all just a friendly supper. I overreacted. No need to rectify the situation. I hear Hever gets booked up early, anyway.
Kind regards
Chloe.

I've obviously hurt the poor woman. She must have taken the Miranda episode very badly indeed. There's not a chance that Hever is booked up. I'll get the tickets anyway. She'll come round. Still, I don't mind saying it left me feeling a bit empty so I decided to retire to the cellar with a glass of Burgundy and ponder Mrs Robinson's idea.

Sheila

What's green and yellow with a wide stripe? Mr Barry's tie, would you believe? And as he waves his baton around, the tie jumps from side to side. I wondered if his wife had told him he's boring. He normally wears grey.

'No, no, no Sopranos; you're late! There's only a semi-quaver before 'Alleluia,' he sang rather loudly. I don't think I've ever seen him get cross before. I couldn't help thinking that if he took his tie off we'd be able to sing much better.

It's funny though, isn't it, how people go grey when they get older. Their hair; their clothes; their skin, even. And for a special occasion they wear beige. George bought a grey sweatshirt the other day. He said it was reduced in the shop in town. I felt somewhat reduced just looking at it.

'Did they have any other colours?' I asked hopefully.

'Possibly, but I like grey. Do you not like it?' he asked.

It's questions like that that I really struggle with. Half of me wants to say, 'No! I hate it! Go and buy a pink one!' but knowing the reaction that would spark the other half of me dutifully says, 'Well, yes it's ok, I suppose.' And even before I get the words out I just know what he's thinking. He's excusing this lacklustre response on *'the tablets'* as he calls it. I don't think he's ever used the word *depression*. I remember when I said to him right at the start of all this, 'the doctor thinks I'm depressed,' he just said, 'well they can cure anything these days with a few tablets,' and went off to his shed.

Marilyn Godber caught me at the end of choir practice and said 'Fancy a coffee? Somewhere on the Green, Food for Thought maybe?'

'Why not,' I replied thinking we'd be overlooking the antique shop where the current owner is having a closing down sale. It was quite busy in the cafe considering it's mid-week. Marilyn managed to point out the sale even before our coffees had arrived, as if I couldn't see for myself.

'Yes, I know.'

'Oh, have you been in?'

'No, no. Our house is full of furniture; what would we want with antiques?'

'Well, you don't have to buy anything; just have a nosey.' She stirred her coffee for the third time. I don't think she even takes sugar. She looked thoughtful so I wasn't too surprised when she said, 'What did you think of Mr Barry's tie, today?'

'Rather off putting, actually.'

'I know what you mean. Whatever possessed him! I think someone should say something.'

'Like what?'

'Well, you know, something on the lines of, after careful consideration and a majority vote, for the sake of the choir and its future, we'd like him to stop wearing brightly coloured ties.'

'And when is this majority vote going to take place?'

''Well, you only had to look at everyone's faces today. And I don't think we've ever sung Handel's Messiah quite so badly.'

'Yes, but that hardly constitutes a secret ballot.'

'I don't care Sheila. Something's got to be said.' She looked at me in a sort of considered way which I found very worrying. I suppose I should have known what was coming.

'You've come on leaps and bounds Sheila, since you first joined us. It really has done you the world of good, hasn't it?' I didn't have time to answer that question before she said, 'I really think you would be the ideal person to approach Mr Barry on the tie issue.'

'No way! I can't do that!'

'Oh!' Marilyn looked surprised. 'Well, I suppose it will have to be me then.'

As we left Food for Thought, she headed straight for The Green Antiques shop. She didn't even ask me if I wanted to join her. Just assumed I would, I suppose. She walked round the shop looking at price tags as if she might seriously buy something. The nice French woman who's selling up was attaching reduced tags to candle sticks. She looked up and smiled at me as if she knew what Marilyn was up to.

'Do you deliver?' Marilyn asked.

'We can do. Where do you live?'

'In the village.'

'Well, no problem then.'

She could have gone on to ask her what she was thinking of buying, but she didn't.

'So what's going to become of this place? After you've gone, I mean?' Marilyn was obviously looking for gossip.

'I believe the new owner intends to keep it as an antique shop.'

I felt like I should explain that David, my son, has bought it and will be moving in with his gay lover and he'll probably wear a lot of pink as he floats round the shop and George will probably have a heart attack and die.

'Well that's good then.' Marilyn said.

'What's good?' I asked.

'Well that it's not going to become a DVD shop or something awful like that.'

'Oh.' I said.

That was Tuesday. As if that wasn't bad enough on Wednesday I had a doctor's appointment for a prescription *review*. Their idea; not mine. I just wanted more anti-depressants to get me through the next few weeks but they said I needed to see the doctor. It was when Dr Jones looked at me earnestly and said 'How are you, Sheila?' I knew it was all going to go terribly wrong. I felt like saying I wasn't coping, it was all too much; Chloe had helped the other night but that was days ago now and it felt like everything was closing in on me.

'I've been OK,' I said, which sounded pathetic, but so did everything else.

'You look brighter,' she said and smiled and then she added, 'how do you feel about coming off the anti-depressants?'

Terrified, was how I felt. But that seemed a bit melodramatic.

'Not sure I'm ready, yet.'

'You're only on a low dose. How about coming off them for a week and see how you get on? The sooner the better really.'

All I could think about was the fact that the whole village was about to discover that the new owner of The Green Antiques is gay and worst of all that includes George.

She was looking at me so I had to say something. 'I'm not sure.'

'Are you still getting out a lot? Trying new things?'

'Oh, yes. I'm still dog-walking, then there's choir and my son's moving back into the village soon. He's bought The Green antiques shop.' That was a really silly thing to say.

'Good! Sounds like now, would be perfect timing.' And then she turned to me as if that was that and it was time to go. No clicks of the mouse, no jerky printer, no green form handed over.

'Right, well I'll see how I get on then,' I heard myself say. She smiled at me as I gathered myself up to go. It was easy for her. Just a simple sentence and a decision made. 'Just try it for a week.' I felt empty walking out. I couldn't even talk to George about it. He thinks I'm already off them.

I wandered out of the surgery; must have been in a daze and without even thinking about it I went up to the church.

Finding myself outside the doors, I decided it would be nice to sit quietly in a pew for a bit. Put off the rest of the day, anyhow. Maureen Gallagher was arranging flowers near the altar, but otherwise it was empty. She simply smiled and nodded but let me be.

Thoughts whirled around my head. How was I before the tablets? Dreadful. How am I now? Not great. And more to the point, how am I going to cope without them? I shouldn't have told the doctor about David. Why didn't I tell her about George? But what would I have said? Still, I'm only on a low dose. That's what *she* said.

'You alright, Sheila?' The vicar appeared from nowhere.
'Oh, yes vicar.' He sat next to me and I realised Maureen had disappeared mid-flower arrangement. The purple gladioli looked quite dramatic in the vase with the leafy green foliage but the yellow roses had yet to make it into the water to brighten it all up.

The vicar sat next to me. We were alone.
'You've chosen a good spot to think it over,' he said with a knowing smile.
'Yes, well, just clearing my head,' I lied. My head had never felt so cluttered; the thoughts ricocheting off the sides of my mind.

He sat perfectly still and said nothing and it reminded me of how Chloe was.
'Challenging times ahead, Sheila?'
'Yes!' I almost pounced on this. It sort of summed it all up without bothering with the difficult detail. He smiled again and I wanted to try and explain.
'David, my son, is moving back to the village.' He's bought, well, he's bought a business here.'
'Is that a good thing?

'Yes and no,' I said and then I decided if there was one person I wasn't going to tell, that my son is gay, it was the vicar.

'Interesting,' he said. I felt all tied up in knots.
'It's George, you see. He doesn't know yet.'
'That your son is moving to the village?'
'Yes.'
'I see,' he said but he might as well have been standing in thick fog. But then somehow he managed to come to my rescue again. 'George and David have had some sort of, falling out? In the past? And that makes it difficult?'

'Yes vicar. That's it.' I said feeling relieved but then I noticed he was looking at me with raised eyebrows. They were so heavily arched his eyes could have been trains coming through tunnels. If only he could bring them down a bit, straighten them out, take the glint out of his eyes, this would all be over. But then I remembered what Chloe had said about it being George's problem, not mine. Every time I reminded myself of that fact I got a wave of relief, even if it was brief.

'You can share anything you wish with me, Sheila. You know that, don't you?'

'Thanks vicar. But really this chat has been most helpful and now I must be on my way. Good afternoon.'

He looked surprised and I decided I could cope with a surprised vicar; it was David's imminent arrival I was struggling with.

Chloe

I might as well have had '*I slept with the CEO of Nourriture Verte'* inscribed across my blouse for all the good I was at work today. I was blushing like a Jane Austen character faced with a naked Darcy emerging from a lake at regular intervals. And I managed to spill not one cup of coffee but two. The first narrowly missed my keyboard which no doubt would have rendered my computer useless until the IT department, conveniently based in Bangalore, managed to replace it. Although I'm not sure what use it was to me today. The second *didn't* miss my white linen trousers. Whatever possessed me to pick that particular garment out of the wardrobe this morning, only a psychotherapist could tell you. Every time I got up from my desk I had to walk with one hand strategically placed over the stain but because it was dangerously close to my crotch, I was left wondering which was the lesser of two evils. I decided to take an early lunch break and dived into Phase Eight where I found a beautiful emerald green silk dress with a price tag one should only glance at. Despite this very obvious transformation the male contingent in the office didn't even manage a bat of an eyelid between them.

    I even, and you won't believe this, hardly noticed handsome young Andrew as he sauntered past my desk. In fact he sort of slowly came into my vision as I gazed across the floor and I thought oh, there's Andrew. It's funny because he smiled at me and then came over and said,

    'Hello Chloe, how's it going?' The glint in his eye was embarrassing.

    Well apart from shagging the CEO of one of my investments and behaving like a teenager it's all going swimmingly, I thought.

    'Great, Andrew. Just great.' A few days previously I would have been mortified with that response but today I seem to be living on another planet and just playing at this real world thing.

'Good, good Chloe,' he said starring at my cleavage and leaning over me to reach for a pen. What on earth is going on? And would you believe he starts scribbling a note.

Fancy a drink in C&B, shall we say 6ish?

I couldn't help recalling that he was dating some bimbo from marketing and I must have looked puzzled because he said, 'No, really!' with this ridiculously earnest look on his face before tripping over my waste paper bin as he departed. Again, back on planet earth a few days ago I'd have swooned and followed him, desperate for attention. Now, well, now I feel like popping him on the arrogant prat shelf along with Alex. What's that expression about buses? I like to think of it as a surplus of chauffeur driven limos actually. After all who wants a bus?

Speaking of arrogant prats, Alex has emailed me several times in the last couple of days. I suppose I do keep replying. It's just too tempting somehow.

To: Chloe
From: Alex
Subject: Much ado about nothing

Dear Chloe,

It's funny isn't it but all that has happened to us could really be summed up with 'Much ado about nothing!' And would you believe I have two tickets for Shakespeare's play of this very title this Saturday at the Lakeside theatre. It would be so lovely if you could join me. We could even laugh at ourselves. After all you've obviously been through some bad times and me too if I'm honest. Let's put it all behind us and have some fun!

Best regards
Alex

....

To: Alex
From: Chloe
Subject: Much ado about hypocrisy

Dear Alex,

What a splendid idea. After all Beatrice and Benedick were just fools to themselves until they saw the light. Looking back at that little incident the other week, it seems so unimportant. Miranda wasn't it? Who turned up during our little get together? She was certainly the stuff of comedy! How I laugh when I think back to how she slapped you round the face, quite violently I seem to remember. What was it she said, 'You two-timing bastard, don't ever come near me again!' Still, she's probably calmed down by now. As you say, much ado about nothing.

I think I'm busy on Saturday.
Chloe

....

To: Chloe
From: Alex
Subject: Delighted you know of the play.

Chloe, darling, it's so refreshing to come across a woman who is so witty, so intelligent, so fun loving and so lonely. I'll pick you up at 6pm on Saturday. I'll do a picnic basket for us both so please don't eat. The forecast is set fair. I can't wait.

Best regards,
Alex

The audacity of the man is quite remarkable. The annoying thing is I have no other plans for this Saturday. I'll have to hide.

    Davina caught me at the end of the day determined to drag me over to Corney & Barrows.
    'You've had sex haven't you? I can tell.'
    'How an earth can you tell?'
    'Ah! So you have!
    'You mean you couldn't tell?'
    'Well I wasn't 100% sure but 90% at least. It was the way you stared at Google all day, without feeling the need to actually search for anything. And when you poured coffee all over yourself, of course.'
    'Oh dear, was it that obvious?'
    'Don't worry darling. Every man in the building is wildly jealous because they know it's not them.'
    'Mm.'
    'Never mind mm. Who was it?'
    'Éduardo Devereux, CEO of Nouritture Verte.' I cringed at myself.
    'Bloody hell Chloe!' She said that rather too loudly and all the so-called jilted men in the office looked round. Davina's eyes looked like they might pop out of her head.
    'Well C&B it is then. I want *all* the detail.'
    'You'll have to form an orderly queue, I've already had an invite from Andrew.'

'Andrew!' Again Davina, bless her, managed to raise her voice so that everyone looked round. 'The two timing...'

'Don't worry! I didn't accept!'

'Thank God for that. You're all mine. Now hurry up. Nice new dress by the way. Bit unsubtle changing at lunch time but still....'

Of course I didn't tell her much. I wasn't really in the mood for socialising. Andrew turned up and looked at me across the bar pretending to be confused. I suppose when you're that devilishly handsome you don't expect women to turn you down even if you do happen to be a two timing twerp. Davina was lovely. I was expecting the Spanish inquisition but after wanting to know the logistics of how it happened (why is that always so important to women?) she was most concerned that I'm OK.

'Usual scenario,' I explained. 'Woman falls for man, man realises and takes her out for dinner, charms her and makes her feel wonderful (if, a little tipsy) so that making love seems like the most natural thing to do.' Davina's pupils were still dilated so I continued.

'My hotel room. Yes he is married. Yes it was wonderful. And no, I'm not seeing him again. Well, not outside the board room at least.'

'Why not?' she asked like all good friends do.

'I'm not sure I even want to,' I said and realised I meant it.

So you see there's not much to tell really, is there? I fell for the charms of a very attractive man. Actually, it's the first time since the divorce. Somehow that does make it significant. All that time spent throwing myself into anything that provided a distraction; work, making my home here in Lodge Lane, trawling round Europe for Green investments, late nights in the office and did I mention work? And without giving men, love or sex or any of that stuff a second thought. Well most of the time, anyway.

And then when I finally succumbed it was in another country so it sort of didn't count. It was far enough away from home to be part of a fairy tale world which has nothing to do with life at home. Or at least I allowed the fantasy to become real without reprimanding myself. After all, the apron strings have been cut long ago; I no longer worry about what Mum would think; I just won't tell her. And the ideal of marriage has been carefully placed in a sealed box marked 'don't bother opening.' The fact is last Wednesday evening as the sun set over the Loire Valley, I suddenly stumbled upon an oasis of excitement, passion and fulfilled desire. Somehow knowing I was getting up in the morning to fly home made it perfect.

But despite all that, the very thought of it was shocking as I sat in the office today. Silly me, what did I look like? I think it's time to put this behind me.

What *am* I going to do about Alex?

Alex

By the time I got to the bottom of the bottle of Burgundy I was really quite excited about the whole idea. I kept telling myself Becky will need a lot of convincing and may well knock it on the head but let's face it she won't be the first woman I've charmed into some venture or other. I've quite enjoyed the hours spent in my garden with her. Oh, and round at Chloe's too. You see we've secretly been looking after her garden whenever she's off on some trip or other. It's not difficult as she leaves her back gate open. Becky was quite horrified by the idea of not telling her initially but I persuaded her that Chloe is too proud to admit she needs help, so we should just get on with it. She seemed to think that she owed Chloe, for one reason or another, so she softened and we've got it rather pretty now, though I say so myself.

It's not bad being in the fresh air. So different to being in an office or stuck in airports waiting for a delayed flight. Anyway I got myself a note pad and wrote the heading 'Plan B'. Then I wrote a list of things that I need to do to research the idea properly. I decided I'd do all this myself before mentioning anything to Becky. It would be so much better to go to her with a rounded business proposition rather than a flaky idea. Having said that, I'll have to avoid the word 'business' of course and use her language, how about:

'Becky, I've thought of a way the two of us can make a bit of money.' That should work, after all the girl's continually financially challenged by her own confession. I've never seen so many cans of baked beans in one cupboard. Thankfully she accepts lunch from me, if offered. So, getting back to the list I wrote:

1. Check out local competition – newsagents' windows, internet (question mark), local papers etc..

2. Find out going hourly rate
3. Buy some books on gardening. Actually I crossed that one out. I'm not sure I can be bothered; Becky seems to know it all.
4. Write business plan – how many clients do we need? etc..
5. Take Mrs R up on offer to be first client. I'll have to play that one carefully with Becky.
6. Transport?

Mm. That could be a tricky one. The Bentley is quite big but not at all suitable for a gardening business. A small van would be ideal. But it's one thing downsizing from a mansion on Oakdene to a cottage in Lodge Lane and entirely another swapping the Bentley for a van. This could be a major stumbling block. Maybe I could get finance from a local bank for a down payment on a van. We could park it outside Becky's house, I'm sure she won't mind; never thought to ask her if she can drive. So that's where I am with this. I haven't come up with a name for the business yet so I'm sticking with Plan B as a kind of working title for now.

Played squash with Freddy last week. He's been so busy with work, and some delightful sounding woman called Penelope, that we haven't met up for a while.
'How's the lovely Miranda?' he asked. I was surprised that he remembered her name.
'I'm sure she's fine; we're not seeing each other anymore.'
'Oh, shame, what happened there? Don't tell me Casanova's been jilted?'
'No, no. Well, not exactly. But actually Freddy, I take exception to the Casanova title.'

'Really! Next thing I know you'll be settling down. That should hit the Times front page, if not Vanity Fair. Eternal bachelor boy marries!'

'Steady on. But you know having some sort of relationship with the right woman wouldn't go amiss right now.'

'Alex Minter-Kemp, is that really you? Ah! I get it. You've met someone haven't you? By God she must be special.'

'You know I think you've hit on something there. Yes, Chloe is rather special.'

'Bloody hell! Tell me more.'

'She lives next door.'

'Convenient.'

'Yes, and works at F&K, Euro Fund desk. Do you know her?'

'By Jove, I think I do. Blonde, long legs, hangs around with Davina, the one with large breasts.'

'Does she now?'

'Well you know I've seen them in C&B a couple of times downing a bottle or two of vino.'

I changed the subject at that point. Felt a little stab to the stomach if I'm honest. It was just too much of a reminder of my old life and it felt weird Chloe still being part of it. After the game, Freddy got a couple of pints in.

'Just for the record what did happen with Miranda?'

'Oh she caught me having supper with Chloe, slapped me round the face and said something on the lines of get lost you bastard.'

'Oh right. Fair enough.'

'So what's the update in the office?'

Must admit, being on the squash court made me realise I'm a bit out of shape. This sedentary lifestyle is taking its toll on my physique so I decided I need to take action. Going to the gym reminds me too much of the old life when I had membership to some classy place in town as part of the job. I really can't afford that now. So when I heard that the woman two doors up walks dogs most days, I thought it might be a good idea to join her. Ideal for a bit of fresh air and exercise. I decided, rather than call round and present the idea to her, I'd try a more subtle approach and just wait till I saw her set off one morning. I found out her name from Becky.

'Morning Sheila,' I said, quite cheerily I thought, as I approached her. She looked concerned.

'Sorry, is this a bad time?' I asked. 'I'm Alex, by the way.'

'Oh well, I'm just off to walk the dogs; I mean other people's dogs, you know, that's what I do.'

'Yes, so I've heard.'

She was still looking at me strangely and I noticed she'd tied a dog lead around her wrist and was pulling at it. I did think seriously about making some banal comment and exiting rather sharpish, but that would have been less than a half hearted attempt, and I'm not one to give up easily.

'Actually, I was wondering if I could be so bold as to join you. You see I just need a bit of exercise.'

'Oh golly. Oh gosh, well I can't see any reason why not,' she said looking like she might strangle herself there and then with the dog lead if it wasn't already cutting off her blood supply at the wrist.

'You know Sheila, please do say if this isn't convenient.' Convenient isn't the right word of course but this woman needed careful handling by the looks of things. So I continued, 'I know I like a bit of solitary myself sometimes. In fact I have a cellar where I go.' Her expression had now moved to horrified. 'What I mean to say is, if you'd prefer to stick with your own company that's entirely OK with me. Really we could forget this conversation ever happened and just get on with our days.'

Finally she smiled. It was such a relief I actually laughed and she laughed too.

'Well, why don't you come along today and we'll see how we get on.'

After that shaky start one could be forgiven for thinking that things could only get better. We had to pick three dogs up first before we could head for the fields. They all seemed friendly enough and Sheila seemed content in their company. I began to feel like I was a major intrusion but once we were on our way she started to make conversation.

'Do you know anything about antiques?' she asked.

'I used to have a house full of them; I suppose I still do but a much smaller house now.'

'Oh, so you had a big house and now you have a small house. Sorry, was that the wrong thing to say?'

'No, no. That's just the way it is. I've down scaled as it were.'

'Not such a bad thing.'

'So what's the interest in antiques?'

'Oh well it's just that my son has bought the Green Antiques shop. He'll be moving in soon.'

'How marvellous,' I said but she looked pale and worried which seemed a bit odd as she'd bought the subject up. 'Lived in Lodge Lane long?' I said changing the subject but still she stared at the ground.

'Yes, we've been here for fourteen years and George, that's my husband, reckons we'll be seeing out our days here.' I wondered if they'd decided on some sort of suicide pact once they reach a certain point. Maybe, once George is too old to perform in the bedroom. Or they've had one too many holidays in Scarborough. Marriage hey, not all it's cracked up to be. You get to Sheila's age, what 55, children flown the nest and all you've to look forward to is planning your own funeral.

'George spends most of his time in the shed, these days, well since he retired.'

'Really? What does he do in the shed?' I couldn't help imagining him plotting 'the End' as it were. Researching the options. How could he make it simultaneous and painless for them both.

'Nothing, as far as I can tell.'

This was even more ominous. If my spouse (hypothetically speaking, of course, God forbid) spent a lot of time in the shed doing nothing I'd be worried.

'Although he does make things.'

That thought sort of hung in the air as we walked along. Actually we were near the top of a hill and I was a bit breathless but more than anything I decided I didn't want to know what George makes in the shed. When we reached the top she looked at me and smiled. 'What do you do Alex?'

I waited until my breathing was even.

'I lost my job in the City a year ago and have recently come to the conclusion that I won't be going back.'

'Oh dear, I'm sorry to hear that.'

'Don't be ridiculous. It's all quite alright. I've actually just started cooking up a Plan B.'

'Oh, I see.' She paused for quite a while before she asked, 'Is Plan B any good?'

'I think so, but we will have to see, only time will tell.'

Chloe said on an email that she thinks she's busy tomorrow evening. This, of course, means she hasn't forgiven me for the Miranda episode yet. I suppose it's taking a bit of a risk getting the picnic ready and just calling on her but I think it's a risk worth taking. I think she's worth it.

Becky

'Come round for dinner,' he says. What was I s'possed to think about that. Alex Minty from next door askin' me round for dinner. Bloody hell!

'I have some rather good steak,' he says. 'And a decent bottle of burgenonny.' Posh wine I s'pose.

'Any particular reason?' I had to ask.

'Well actually there's something I wish to discuss with you.' Well that was pretty undercover but I didn't want to look like I was desperate to know so I just said,

'Oh, OK then.' All cool like.

I was lookin' at him the other day as he was diggin' a patch at the back of his. He's not bad lookin' although whatever that bugenonny stuff is I bet it's the cause of him putting on a bit of weight. I don't fancy him. Of course I don't. He's got amazing blue eyes that you can't help noticin' but he's just not my type. I mean we'd need a transient person so we knew what each other was sayin' half the time. But anyway I thought it's been a long time since I 'ad steak so it's worth it just for that.

I put on a skirt; well he's never seen me in anythin' but my jeans and scruffs. But I do actually have a skirt so I thought I might as well wear it. Sheila said she'd baby sit for little Jack so he could sleep in his own bed. She actually seemed to really want to do it. I said it was alright if she wanted her husband to join her, they could treat the place like their own for the evening but she said,

'Oh, no it's OK; I'll happily do it on my own. And just let me know, any time.'

I can only think, when you get to that age you just wanna stay in and watch the telly. Anyway so I turns up and he looks at me a bit strange but then he said,

'Good evening Becky, it's good to see you.'

And I thought, well you did ask me, so don't pretend you didn't. I don't normally go round me neighbour's house all dressed up on the off chance they wanna feed me. But I thought best keep things friendly so I said.

'Good of you to invite me, actually.'

He smiled at me, a really big smile and I thought what's all that about?

It looked like he'd tidied up a bit and the dining table was laid with knives and forks and there was this folder on there which seemed a bit odd. He poured me a glass of red wine and handed it to me.

'Try that,' he said.

Well I drank some and I thought that's pretty amazing; I could drink a lot more of that.

'Not bad,' I said and he grinned at me and then he said, 'Good, good, I'm glad you like it. Dinner won't be long.'

As we ate the dinner it was kinda of a weird situation 'cos normally we're out in the garden and we don't talk that much and he started askin' me things which I haven't felt the need to tell him about before.

'So, how long have you lived in Lodge Lane, Becky?'

'Just over a year now. Mrs Barnes, she's my landlady, she's ever so nice actually and I think she took pity on me and decided it would be better for me to live somewhere decent after all.' I sort of stopped there, thinking that maybe I was saying too much. Alex did look a bit puzzled at first but then he just smiled and said, 'I had a pretty rough time before I came here. But somehow I feel my fortunes are changing.' It's hard to believe that Alex could have been through a rough patch and I didn't like to ask what all that was about but then he said,

'You see Becky I used to work up in the City.'

'What like Chloe does?'

'Yes, exactly. Well pretty similar anyway. The point being, I was made redundant and haven't worked since. That was a year ago.'

'Blimey you do well out of the social!' I said but then wished I hadn't but luckily he laughed.

'It's nothing to do with social security. I downsized when I came here.'

I wondered if he meant he'd cut down on food but he looked healthy enough.

'What I mean is I used to live in rather a large house and I sold it to release the capital and bought this place to live in.'

'I got some of that but what the hell is release the capital?'

'Well, put simply,' he looked at me and after a bit he said, 'well actually it's just a way of making a bit of money.'

I suddenly thought this must be what the evening was all about. Alex was going to tell me I secretly had some capital to be released somewhere and me and little Jack will come into some money and will be able to eat steak for the rest of our lives. After all I've never understood money. And by the way the steak was bloody fantastic much better than I've ever had in a Berni Inn.

'Sounds interesting,' I said.

'Well it's just the way it is,' he said.

'What do you mean?' I had to ask.

'It doesn't matter.' He looked a bit uncomfortable but then he said, 'What brought *you* to Lodge Lane?'

It would have been so easy to say, a husband who abused me, a social worker who took pity on me and a landlady who was ever so nice and that's about it. But somehow I couldn't tell Alex about all that.

'It just happened, you know. Jack and I needed to be in a better place and here we are and thank God for that. There's nothing else to say really.'

He went quiet for a bit but then he said, 'Well I'm glad you're alright now. More wine?'

After we'd eaten and I suppose drunk all the wine, Alex picked up the folder and I thought here we go, this is what all this is about.

'Becky, I hope you don't mind but I've been doing a bit of research into an idea.' Were we back to revealing capitals?

He went on, 'Do you remember Mrs Robinson's suggestion about us gardening for her and other people?'

'Well yes, I remember her saying she'd rather pay us than anyone else.'

'Exactly. 'I've been looking into it and I think there are a lot of people in this area who would gladly pay a gardener to keep their gardens looking tidy.'

'You don't mean they'd actually pay the likes of you and me, do you?'

'Well yes; why not? Sheila next door is paid by local people to walk their dogs while they are at work all day. You see they have busy lives, no time for dog walking and no time for gardening.'

'So they wouldn't be watchin' us then?'

'Well, I doubt it. But even if the odd occasion arose when they were, we have nothing to hide. Look what we've managed to do to with my little patch.'

'Yeah, it's not bad now is it, when you think what it was like.'

'Exactly! Now.' he took the papers out of the folder and started shuffling them around, laying some out on the table. There must have been twenty sheets or more and I thought how on earth did he manage to fill all that paper with words about doin' a bit of gardening.

'You see here Becky, I've worked out, based on the going hourly rate, that the two of us could make a decent living.'

Well I don't mind telling you the figures were enough to make my eyes pop out of my head compared to what I get on the Social. But still who knows if we can pull this off.

'But would I lose all me benefits?'

'Well I'm not sure Becky but if you like I can help you with that.' And that made me think that this man is actually a very nice man. He really has thought of everything, scribbling away on all these sheets of paper; must have taken him ages.

'I will need to make sure little Jack is looked after.'

'Of course,' he said as if he'd thought of that as well.

'And we'll need transport, of course,' he said picking up another bottle of wine but then putting it back again.

'Well thank God for the Bentley,' I said but he looked a bit surprised. Of course it's his pride and joy. He doesn't want soil all over his leather seats.

'I was thinking of a small van.'

'I can't imagine you in a van.'

'No, well it's going to require quite a few changes this whole business. I don't suppose you drive, do you?'

'It's been a while; I've never had me own car.'

'But you've passed your test?

'No, I haven't. Failed it once but I can drive.'

'Perhaps a few lessons then?'

'You offering, Alex?'

'Well, we'll have to see.'

'Be a shame to have to sell the Bentley.'

'Oh no! I'm not going to do that!' He looked quite put out like I'd suggested he had an arm off.

'No, I was thinking of finding a way of acquiring a van.'

How on earth do you acquire a van? I can't imagine him nicking one. But as he made the coffee I sat back and I felt quite excited by it all but at the same time scared. It's just something I've not done before. But when I think of all the times I've been driven half crazy by not havin' any money and lookin' after little Jack all on my own I just think something's got to happen, whatever it is, something's got to change. Maybe this is it.

Sheila was laughing at the television when I got home.
'Everything alright?'
'Oh yes love, Jack's sound asleep, no bother at all.'
'Oh, thanks ever so.'
'It was a pleasure Becky. Did you have a good evening?'
'Well it was different, I'll tell you that.'
'Sometimes different is good,' she said as she went home next door.

I went straight up to look at Jack; he's like an angel when he sleeps. I wondered if Sheila had noticed that his blanket is wearing a bit thin and there's a stain on it which I've never managed to get out. But *he* doesn't notice and he's warm enough, so it does for now, anyway. It's funny isn't it, it seems there are some people in this world who have revealing capital and some people who don't.

And I thought about what Alex had said about us setting up a business together and earning lots of money and I decided I really wanted it. I want it so much. To have enough money to give me and Jack a better life. And why the hell shouldn't I?

Sheila

George makes little packages with his food. A bit of beef, a bit of carrot, a bit of Yorkshire pudding and then he scoops up as much gravy as he can before whooshing the whole lot up to his mouth. Of course some of the gravy doesn't make it and occasionally a bit of carrot can't cling to the fork any longer and crash lands back on the plate but on the whole it's quite successful. And he chews well. My father always said, 'chew your food well Sheila,' never giving any kind of explanation as to why.

    He was away a lot. My mum would say, 'he's on conference; back Friday; shall we make him a special tea?' I never answered that question but she always did make an effort on his return. I just loved the times when he was away. Mum made us our favourite meals and we were allowed to watch television for an hour after, maybe more. She sat between me and my sister on the sofa and we all cuddled together. The special tea for Dad was a rigid affair; no elbows on the table; don't speak unless you want a short answer, no leaving any food on your plate. He didn't talk much about his time away, only a little to Mum and not in language I understood anyway. Mum always nodded and smiled but I wonder now if she was listening. It was Dad who decided when the meal was over retiring to his study to 'catch up on things' as he put it.

    George seems to digest his food well, without any problems; a sign of a contented man without a worry in the world. I didn't touch mine; didn't even pretend I was going to eat it. The very smell of it made me feel sick.

    'You're not eating yours,' George told me.

    'No.' The fights gone out of me; the need to explain has disappeared. After all I don't understand what's going on myself.

    'What's wrong? Are you not well?' I could have spoken his lines for him.

'I just don't feel like a roast right now.'

'Oh, you're going to eat it later are you?' I hadn't answered before he said, 'Are you sure there's nothing wrong? Should you see a Doctor?

To George, Doctors are the font of all knowledge, the answer to any dilemma life might throw at you; their words form the blue print of his life. Finally the last parcel was chewed and swallowed and George hesitated before he got up. I managed a small smile so that he could convince himself that things were OK.

'I think I'll read the paper,' he said and had made it to the back door before he shouted, 'in the shed.'

As soon as he'd gone I went into the kitchen and slid the contents of my plate into the bin. I opened the cupboard doors and there, almost beckoning me was a packet of custard powder. Pouring milk into a jug I decided to make a pint and as I stirred the mixture over the hob the sweet smell turned my appetite from revulsion to craving in a way I couldn't possibly explain. After an agonising couple of minutes to wait for it to cool down I was in heaven.

It's three 'o' clock in the morning and I'm ironing. Yesterday I did the two 'til five shift in the land of the wide awake while everyone else sleeps. And tonight I made it to 2.45 convincing myself this is a slight improvement. At least I've given up the hour of pretence before I get up. The hour of willing myself to sleep, trying to focus on calm thoughts and my shallow breath but instead being drowned out by George's snoring. The thought of David moving in to the village and George still not knowing hammers at my mind relentlessly. All the reasons why it will be OK come and go, each attempting to soften the blows, but ultimately fail.

My sister called; she's recovering from an operation and I nearly said 'I'll come and stay for a few days; help you out.

The thought of running away from Lodge Lane is very tempting. I would be in a safe place where no one could get me. I wouldn't have to meet David and his lover with smiles and pleasantries while I fathom out how I'm going to cope with this new situation in my life. George could discover his son for himself and deal with his own prejudices without blaming me because I just wouldn't be there to blame. Marianne from the choir could let her curiosity get the better of her and go and have a look at the new owners of the Green Antiques and realising it is run by two gay guys decide she's not buying anything today, thank you. She may even discover one of the offenders is my son. Sheila Gifford's son! Now that would throw her into turmoil. I can imagine her first thought would be to find a way to oust me from the choir. A secret ballot would be arranged probably so secret no one else would know about it. She'd simply read out the guilty as charged notice and check the expressions of all the choristers' faces. Each look of surprise or horror would register a yes vote. I might as well be labelled a witch heading for the ducking chair!

I've just remembered the hard single bed in my sister's tiny spare bedroom and the restless nights I've had on it. There's no way I can do the night shift closeted in her tiny home, well not unless she generates a hell of a lot of ironing.

Speaking of which, this is the last of George's shirts. I iron the sleeves first and then the collar, yoke, front and back. Each time I turn the shirt from sleeve to collar I can hear my mother's voice, 'collar first Sheila.' That was the way she did my Dad's shirts. She was set in her ways. I suppose I am too but at least it's a different way. There's not much more to do now. Maybe I should take in other people's ironing. I could make a bit of money and add it to the dog walking fund. I could call it the wide awake club fund. I've never really thought what I'll do with that money. It's not much really but it's more than I've ever had that I can call *mine*. I've ironed the table cloth, all my dog walking trousers that I don't normally iron and every napkin in the house. 22 in total. Goodness knows why we've got 22 napkins. The ones we have fit flat on the board so you don't have to move them about. I fold them lightly twice into a square and place them onto the pile. The monotony of doing 22 seems to induce tiredness so lately I've encouraged the liberal use of napkins at every opportunity. George looks at me as if I'm mad (and I'm beginning to think I am) but he doesn't say anything. With the last one folded, I feel as though if there's any kind of God up there he'll let me sleep.

The pinkness of the spare room always makes me smile. When we decorated it George said, 'Why pink? I don't like pink; pink's for a girl.' As we've been married for twenty four years I didn't need to say anything, I just bought the paint.

It's become part of my ritual now to come in here with a mug of warm milk and sit up in bed sipping in anticipation of finally going back to sleep. And when my head hits the pillow I'll have got to that stage where I don't care if I sleep or not, so I probably will.

Chloe

It is amazing; gets me every time. You're wandering through these romantic Italian gardens with erotic statues and giant urns emerging at every turn and suddenly, there it is. A lake so vast and so still with weeping willows dipping their branches in. It looks like it goes on forever, into the horizon, but of course it doesn't. I looked round and realised that Alex was staring at me. He must have appreciated how moved I was. Probably thought it was his presence but of course it's just this place. He spoke.

'Quite something, isn't it? I bet, well - I hope you're glad you came now?'

I didn't want to go, of course. Why would I want to spend an evening with this deluded womaniser! But with nothing else planned, and *Much ado about nothing* actually being a favourite play of mine and this being a chance to see it live in such a stunning setting, well, surely that's reason enough to come along?

Even so, he hadn't even popped round to confirm so I was doubtful all day as to what would happen. But just in case I made sure I was ready on time. Anyway when six 'o clock came round, there was a loud knock at the front door. I found myself stood still in my bare feet on the inside of the door while he stood on the outside. It was quite strange really because it was only then that I realised that I'd actually made quite an effort. The green silk dress I was wearing, well I'd picked it up from the dry cleaners that very morning; my freshly painted toe nails looked ful and my gorgeous Jimmy Choo sandals were just waiting by the door for my feet to wriggle into them. I have to admit I had my finest underwear on, not that it mattered really but it makes me feel good and with this kind of difficult evening ahead you need all the help you can get. A cream pashmina was conveniently draped over a chair in the hallway ready for me to grab on my way out which I realised was now - but still I left it there. I imagined Alex stood there just a few feet away but with a solid oak door between us it seemed safe to think of his piercing blue eyes and his blonde hair combed back smartly for the occasion. I decided he'd be dressed in pressed chinos and a stripy shirt, a look that was on the smart side of casual (and by the way I wasn't wrong). And I'm sure I could smell a heady pungent aftershave through the letterbox. And so I stood there, zen, as they say, in the moment. Part of me wanted to fling the door wide and lunge into the inevitable and the other part wanted to retreat away to my cosy world of home alone. Despite this delay he hadn't knocked for a second time which was very annoying and so eventually I gave in. I picked up my Jimmy Choos and sneaked as quietly as I could back into the living room. Then with my naked feet firmly in place I clanked my heels back to the front door to fling it open.

'Hello Alex,' I said and his eyes smothered every inch of me with a victorious smile.

'Good evening Chloe!'

The roof was down on a creamy polished Bentley and a delightful picnic basket sat on the back seat. 'Shall we go then?' I said, feeling as though my fate was sealed.

'Did you want to take your pashmina?' he asked. Not only had he noticed it, but he was thoughtful enough to remind me to take it!

'Oh yes.' I grabbed it wondering how I was ever supposed to hate this man. Consistently, that is.

'It really is lovely, this place,' was all I allowed him as we walked away from the foot of the lake and found a place to picnic. The basket he had prepared was a delight with fruits, cheeses and fresh breads and a heady Rioja which seemed to relax every muscle in my body and probably my mind as well. Surprisingly the conversation was easy.

'How's life at F&C?' he asked. I thought about Nourriture Verte's plunging share price, an otherwise lacklustre fund, Andrew's recent curious attentions and the crazy passionate coupling with Eduardo.

'Not without its challenges.'

'Tell me more,' his eyes lit up and I quite liked the genuine interest. As an ex City boy he really knows his stuff and he actually had some sound advice for me and all went well until eventually he said, 'I suppose a job like yours doesn't leave you time for much else?'

I didn't want to say it but it slipped out. 'There's isn't much else.' As if that wasn't bad enough I felt the need to explain. 'I was married, you see.'

'Oh dear,' he said but then quickly followed by 'I mean, oh dear, if it didn't last.'

'Oh dear all round, really; all a bit of a disaster! We lasted three years.'

'Well, good effort; I've not even made it up the aisle!' It was at that moment that I told myself, Chloe, don't ever get involved with this man.

'So confirmed bachelor?' It felt safe to cast this judgement now in jovial fashion. Trouble was, he thought about it.

'You know I wouldn't have hesitated to answer that question a year ago but now - well let's just say I think I've changed a lot and who knows what will happen.'
That was confusing. What was I supposed to think now? Why couldn't he have said he was more likely to saw his Bentley in half than tie the knot.

'Two minutes to take our seats,' he announced and I decided the only thing to do was to lose myself in Shakespeare. Beatrice was a star! How I admire her. So clever; so witty; it's almost hard to believe she falls for Benedick in the end but of course this is Shakespeare doing romance not tragedy. Alex laughed in all the same places as me. Curious. He seemed quite moved at the end, a bit like me at the lake.

I've decided to be very grown up about all this and admit to myself that I actually do fancy him. I know, it's hard to believe but I do. And the good thing is after all I've been through with David and the divorce and all that, well - I know what I want and I know that I don't want Alex. He lacks depth. That's what it is. I mean he's just out for what he can get from women, any woman, doesn't matter. I bet he thought taking me to such a beautiful romantic place would persuade me to sleep with him. Huh! It takes a lot more than that to win me over. (Actually Éduardo in France was of course a bit of an exception; let's just call it a blot on an otherwise pure landscape.)

I can't say that I didn't thoroughly enjoy the evening but then given delicious food and wine and a fine play I would expect to have a pretty good time. And it was one of those lovely summer evenings when it stays warm well into the night and we drove back to Lodge Lane with the roof down. And it made me smile. I felt heady with joy for no particular reason and I was almost disappointed when we arrived home. He parked up and opened my door for me.

'Thank you Alex. That was a lovely evening.' I stepped out of the car and found myself stood next to him.

'I'm so glad you enjoyed it.'

And we just looked at each other, until we realised we were looking at each other and so looked away. And then we just stood there for quite a while and not even the moon spoke. I was waiting for 'Let's do it again sometime,' even though I don't want to, you have to expect this kind of comment after a guy has taken you out. A smile crept across his face and I think I must have smiled too but that was just the wine earlier.

'Dearest Chloe; your company is a joy,' he said and his hand brushed my cheek and rested on the back of my head and before I knew it he had kissed me firmly on the lips. 'Goodnight,' he said and walked away.

Somehow this seemed quite OK. The sort of behaviour you'd expect from a gentleman on a first date. But Alex, a gentleman? It must have been midnight when I closed my front door behind me but I didn't want to go to bed; I don't think I wanted the day to end. I threw off my sandals, managed to find a bottle of Rioja, poured myself a glass and sipped it on the sofa reliving the evening moment by moment with a smile on my face.

Alex

Sunday. Bloody Sunday. I woke up full of the joys after Saturday evening. Woke up alone, you understand. Yes, I've decided to play the long game with Chloe. Think I quite surprised her actually. And you know it was terribly difficult keeping my hands off her. She looked sexier than ever stood by that lake. But I just had this resounding feeling that if I pounced she would reject me and then where would we be?

Anyway Sunday turned out to be one of those days when you start off completely deluded with optimism only to find yourself at the end of the day feeling empty and verging on depressed. My parents came for lunch. Enough said you might be thinking.

'Just to see the place; see where you're living these days,' my mother had said on the phone. It's been a couple of months now since I moved in and I was beginning to think that they just wouldn't come. But then I got the call and so I thought, better make an effort.

'I'll do lunch; just a roast,' I said thinking about an excellent Claret that my father would like and that would go rather well with beef.

'Oh, no need to bother,' Mum said followed by 'See you lunchtime, then.' She's always managed to confuse me. The times I've been mid-frown or mid-puzzling thought as she cuts me off. But still I bought the beef and a few vegetables and made sure the Claret had time to breathe; what a fool I was to think it might have gone OK.

I watched them arrive from the window as the travesty unfolded. Their Jaguar, always polished to perfection; beige leather seats and probably the most over-serviced car you're likely to find, crept cautiously up Lodge Lane as if entering enemy territory. Father moved his glasses up his nose so that he could peer out to discover how the commoners live. The look of disdain on his face didn't move. Mum got out of the car, brushed herself down and tiptoed to my door. Luckily as it was a short distance, she didn't manage to catch anything. By the time I opened up my dear little home to them they were both in a state of deep shock. I did think that maybe I should just dial 999 and have them carried away to intensive care to get over the short but appalling experience. It was as if they hadn't expected *me* to answer the door. Perhaps it had all been a terrible mistake and actually I still lived back at Oakdene.

'Hello Mum, Dad, good to see you,' I said in some ridiculous upbeat tone as if I was trying to drag them up from the depths of despair.

'Son,' my Dad said vaguely. Well at least he still recognises me.

'Alex,' my Mum managed. 'So this is where you live now.' Always a useful reminder, I find.

'Yes, yes, do come in.'

Dad wandered into the living room looking bemused and turned around several times as if he was looking for something; probably another 20 feet.

'Shall I take your coat?'

'Ah, yes.' As he struggled out of it he looked old, probably because he is, but I couldn't help thinking that the events of the last year had only served to accelerate the process and, of course, that's all my fault. It was at that moment that I happened to glance through the window and caught sight of Chloe. She must have been walking into the village; the sun was shining and suddenly I felt trapped. I watched her, even waved but she didn't turn round but walked purposefully onwards. Maybe I'm deluding myself about her as well?

My mother returned having already completed the petite tour of the downstairs.

'It's much smaller than your last place, isn't it?'

Dad reared his head, 'What do you expect Margaret? The boy's been out of work for twelve months!'

Forty nine. I'm forty nine and my father still thinks of me as a boy, and one that is oblivious to hurtful comments. There was so much I *wanted* to say to them; so much I've already tried to explain bit by bit but now I know with resounding certainty that it is, *useless*.

'Lunch will be ready soon,' I said trying to move the afternoon on.

'It smells good,' my mother said and I felt quite chuffed, just for a moment.

'It's such a shame you didn't marry, Alex dear; you'd have a wife to cook for us instead of having to do it yourself.'

I dragged myself into the kitchen wondering how much more of this farce I could take.

With lunch served I hoped that maybe we could all relax. The conversation might flow with the wine but father simply said,

'As I'm driving I won't be able to enjoy the Claret.'

I was going to tell them about Becky and setting up the gardening business. I had even thought about mentioning Chloe, just describing her as a friendly neighbour and remarking on our soiree at Hever Castle. But the fact is father can't comprehend me doing anything but going back to the City. He still asks about Freddy and the old crowd. He's stuck in my past. He even said, 'when you get back to Oakdene,' and for the first time, I realised, that I wouldn't even want to go back.

The rest of the afternoon was a series of delights. My father spilt gravy on his suit trousers halfway through the meal and this caused much commotion. Mother looked at the four walls of my kitchen, each in turn, twice and sighed. Words obviously failed her. They told me about how my sister is expecting her third child and how wonderful that is and at that point my father even smiled. Oh yes and how her husband with his rock solid job in accountancy has just received promotion. And then they left. I wonder if they'll ever return. But you know somehow, inside, I managed to smile through the whole ridiculous affair and for one reason only, Chloe.

As soon as I saw the Jaguar turn out of Lodge Lane I threw my jacket on and strolled into the village to catch the last of the afternoon sun. I don't know why I thought Chloe would still be there. But there was a chance and somehow bumping into her seemed less intrusive than knocking on her door. When I got home the house seemed empty and I decided to send her an email. I simply said, 'Dear Chloe, I enjoyed Saturday evening immensely. I can only hope that you did too.' Two simple sentences trying to reach out to her but do they go far enough? As I hit the send button I felt hollow.

Monday morning at least brought hope. When I woke up I wanted to embrace the day. I've got a business to run, I thought to myself! I must admit that thought forced a wry smile. But after a year of rolling over and going back to sleep, mainly to put off the inevitable dawning of a new jobless day, I actually felt that there was a purpose to this a *working* day! Becky and I, or should I say 'The Green Machine', as we've called our business have our first proper gardening assignment. Somehow it feels like a hurdle to be leapt, probably one of many, but the prize at the end might be... well, we'll see.

Becky

It must have been a week ago now. Alex comes round first thing Monday morning, like we're in some sort of hurry all of a sudden and says 'Come on, we've got our first assignment.' I looked at him and he was wearin' the clothes he has on when we're gardening so I figured that's what assignment means.

'But Jack's not at playgroup today.'

'Bring him with you,' he said as if that was just ever so simple. His car engine was already running!

'He needs a car seat.'

'I've fitted one in the back.' Blimey, I thought! What's come over him? That was pretty amazing that we could take little Jack in the Bentley.

'Well it's a good job too,' I said. 'Give me five minutes.' He looked really put out. What does he think I am; sittin' by the front door waiting to be called for gardenin'. I actually needed longer than five minutes as gettin' little Jack ready is never easy but I just grabbed everything I thought we needed and shoved it in an old bag. Alex didn't even look at the bag, just tossed it in the boot. Luckily Jack was so amazed he was goin' in this funny shaped car that he didn't make a fuss. We was all belted up and I looked at Alex and I was wonderin' where the spades and stuff were going to go.

'Mrs Francis-Williams has her own tools; they're in the shed; I've got the key.' Well blow me down if he can't read my mind now. Hard to believe he used to live in a big house and now he's hangin' round with the likes of me.

'Bleedin' marvellous,' I said and I s'pose that sounded a bit ungrateful but it was only 'cos he was in a strange mood that I said it like that. But then when I looked at him properly I thought he wasn't lookin' too bright so I felt a bit bad.

'You alright?' I asked trying to sound like I didn't care.

'Of course I am,' he said so I knew that he was in one of those cave moods that men have. My friend told me about it once when I first started havin' problems with Eddie. Apparently men like to go into caves sometimes when they've got problems and stay there until they've worked it out. If they don't go, they're just bleedin' angry but don't say anythin'. But then before I knew it we've pulled up to this big posh house, even posher than Mrs Robinson's, with one of those gravel drives. Alex parked up and turned off the engine but instead of gettin' out of the car he sat back and said nothing. I didn't know what to do but then he turned and smiled at me and said,

'Becky, this is our first proper gardening job.'

Of course I know that, but I also sort of knew why he said it. It was kinda one of those moments you might remember when you're old like Mrs Robinson; she was always one for resolving. I looked at him and I thought, bleedin' hell, he's going to burst into tears next!

'That's a good thing isn't it?' I thought it best to point out just in case he was rushin' off to another cave somewhere.

'Yes, of course it is, Becky. Thank you.'

'But *you* set it up.'

'No Becky, *you* were my inspiration.'

Well no one's ever called me their inspiration before and I thought, Becky, you might be crap at most things but if you're an inspiration then you must be doing something right.'

The house looked like it was mainly for show and if you lived there you'd be a nervous wreck worrying about making a mess or breakin' something. Mrs Double Jar Whatsit had left a note on the shed door which said 'The Gardener' on it. Alex didn't look very pleased but opened it and read out:

Gone to cricket with Mr F-W. Everything you need in shed. Mrs F-W.

I was quite relieved she wasn't around what with having little Jack with us and he was already running round this enormous great lawn like he wants to cover every bit of it. The stupid thing was the garden was just as bad as the house! A lawn like a putting green, borders that looked like they had to be in by 10 'o' clock in case they caught a cold and trees that were snipped at daily so that they stayed in a proper tree shape and just in case a branch strayed out of place. It was like someone had just been and we were too late. I found myself wandering around in circles wondering what on earth we were supposed to do and Alex was doing the same. Each time I spotted a deadhead or a weed I thought bingo but I was never going to reach full house. Then Alex and I backed straight into each other but neither of us giggled. 'Three hours.' he said, 'she wants us to do three hours a week.'

'I suppose we could always talk to the plants, like Prince Charlie does, give them a bit of encouragement.' Alex smiled at that and said, 'it is rather perfect isn't it?'

'The woman's doolally if you ask me!'

'Well don't complain, she's paying us £60 an hour.'

'Sixty quid an hour; she's mental!'

Turns out the three hours of trying to find something to do were nearly up when Mrs la de da turns up. She's standin' there in front of her posh French windows holding a tray and shouts, 'drinks and snacks!' I wondered if she's got a couple of dogs. Alex waved and called to her, 'Hello Mrs Francis-Williams. Be over in a tick.' Such a polite boy. I suddenly remembered Jack but realised she couldn't see him because he was playing with his toys behind a massive hedge.

By the time we got down to the patio she'd gone, thank God. Turns out that the drinks is lemonade and the snacks is raw cauliflower. Yuk, I thought but Alex was brave enough to chomp his way through a piece.

The next day we went from the blimey to the ridiculous. Some bloke called Derek had rung Alex wanting to know how much we'd charge him to sort out his garden. We gets round there and it's pouring with rain and we're all standin' around getting really wet lookin' at this mound of mud. It looks like he's never bothered with it at all. I only spotted a few shrubs that were all sprawley 'cos they'd never been cut back.

'The wife wanted a pond, you see,' the man said.

'Really?' Alex said 'cos he's polite.

Well there's no bleedin' pond unless you count the big puddle at the bottom of the mud heap so I don't know what's goin' on 'ere.

'Does she still want a pond?' I had to ask.

'Actually she's left me.'

I made sure I didn't look at Alex and heard him cough a lot before he said,

'I'm sorry to hear that.'

I wondered if he was hoping that if we made his garden all lovely, with a pond of course, his wife would come running back, 'Oh Derek, now we've got a pond I love you again and want to be with you forever!'

'Well there's certainly quite a bit to do' Alex said.

'Expensive, will it be?' he looked worried.

'I'll have to consult my partner, if you could leave us for a moment.'

'Oh, yes, of course, cup of tea?'

'Lovely.'

With Derek out the way Alex said. 'What do you reckon? It'll take a few days to sort this lot out, won't it?' I liked the way he turned to me wanting my advice; that made me feel good.

'Too right. I mean we're not Groundforce.'

'No, we're not miracle force either.' Alex said scratching his head.

'And I think it's a miracle he's after if he's expecting his wife back!'

Alex smiled. 'I don't know Becky, we thought we were setting up a gardening business; turns out we're marriage guidance now!' And then we laughed together and for a minute I forgot it was raining and my feet were soaking wet.

We drank our tea in the rain as we had muddy boots on so we weren't allowed in the house. By then I couldn't have got any wetter. Alex said he'd do the man a quote but it would take a few days' work and he seemed OK with that. On the way home we laughed and laughed and Alex didn't even seem to mind that we were messing up his beautiful car just sitting in it. I picked Jack up from playgroup and squeezed him. 'It's all goin' to be all right' I said into his little ear.

Wednesday the sun shone but there was no work and Jack got a bit bored even though we could go in the garden. It almost seemed wrong doing my own when we could be getting paid to do someone else's. Thursday was the same. And Friday. By Saturday morning I couldn't bear it any longer so I knocked on Alex's door. He opened it and for a moment he didn't say anything which made me worried.

'Hello Becky, how are you?'

'I'm OK. You?'

'Yes. Yes, I'm fine.'

'Well that's good then. I won't trouble you,' I said 'cos I thought he might be back in his cave.

'No, no don't be silly. Come in for a coffee. I've made some fresh.'

We sat at the kitchen table.

Alex poured the coffee and said, 'Derek, the man wanting a pond, said we were too expensive.'

'Oh.'

'You see since his wife left he's struggled a bit financially.'

'My heart bleeds.'

'So I said we could do it for less.'

'Good for you! Anything to keep us busy.'

'Oh, good, I'm glad you agree.' He looked relieved and I was really touched the way he cared what I thought.

He stared into his coffee for a bit before he said, 'You know there's bound to be ups and downs with this business.'

'Alex, mate, my life's been downs and downs for years; any ups are just a bloody bonus!' And we both laughed and it was like we were back in the Bentley soaking wet and the last three days hadn't happened.

George

I spotted it in the charity shop. An airfix model of the Cutty Sark. Number of pieces 220; skill level 4 for the more experienced modeller. 'Never been used' the label stuck on the side said.

'Is it all there?' I asked the woman at the counter. She looked at me as if that was a stupid question and I suppose it was.

'Twenty five pounds, please,' she said. And you can't argue with that; these are hard to find these days.

When the children were young I made quite a few. David would always want to help me. It's delicate work of course and his little fingers were just the job.

'Dad, can I put the mast in? Please Dad?'

'Go on then son. Steady as she goes,' I would say and he always repeated me with a look of intense concentration on his face, 'Steady as she goes.'

Anyway I took the box into the shed, cleared a space on the workbench and poured myself a cup of tea from the flask. This was going to be the start of hours of losing myself in another world; I couldn't wait. After all keeping out of Sheila's way is a good thing these days. She seems to have gone from bad to worse; I just don't understand her. But, of course, that was before I knew what was going on.

Day after day I found time to work on the model. Sometimes I didn't know why I was doing it but it just felt good and it kept me out of the house; body and mind occupied, engaged in activity; after all that's what it's all about isn't it? You could be forgiven for thinking that, if you kept up with my wife!

Bit by bit the ship formed and I almost didn't want to finish it. But finally it was all complete; everything in its place and painted just as it should be. She looked beautiful. I couldn't help admiring it; it was my pride and joy. I even said 'steady as she goes' as I put the mast in and it made me smile and well, a tear crept into the corner of my eye. I looked at it for some time admiring its intricacy and its beauty and feeling really pleased with myself. I found a special place for it on the shelf in the shed so that I could see it from the old armchair when I sat and had my cup of tea in the afternoons.

But of course, all that was before, before I knew about David. To be confronted with an overt queer with something to prove is one thing. To realise he's living in *your* village with *your* son is...

It's like he's invaded our space; the space we were happy in. Why did he have to come to Hartfield?

'Why shouldn't he come back to his own village?' Sheila argued.

'I suppose you think this is all OK? This is *just fine!*'

'Well yes, I do actually.'

'You knew didn't you? You knew all along!'

'He told me on the phone a while ago.'

'And you thought *what* exactly?'

'I thought a lot of things actually but mainly that you would react like this; fly off the handle.'

'Too bloody right! It's bad enough David being the way he is without flaunting it under my nose!'

'Isn't it time you accepted him. Isn't it time you accepted that your son is gay.'

'I'll never accept that!'

'Don't be ridiculous.'

'Why, why couldn't he stay away?'

'Out of sight,' she said quietly. It was like she was in control and it made my blood boil.

Where did it all go wrong? I had a good career, I provided well for my family; Sheila doesn't want for anything. I thought retiring early was for the best, how wrong can you be? How was I supposed to know my wife was going to turn into some custard-craving insomniac, hell bent on plotting with her son to destroy our lives.

Suddenly everything was for nothing. I just felt rage. I stormed into the shed and as soon as I saw the ship I knew I couldn't bear to look at it for a second longer. I grabbed it, lay it on the work bench and took my hammer to it because my bear hands just weren't enough. I crashed down on it over and over again until there were bits everywhere and the mast was in pieces and you would never have known what it was meant to be. It was just a mess, any mess to be swept away. I brushed the pieces onto the floor with my arm and stared down at them in disbelief. And then I cried. My shed; my refuge, destroyed.

Chloe

Davina plonked a glass of Chablis in front of me and announced to most of Corney and Barrows, 'well it doesn't get better than this, darling!'

'Sh. What do you mean? I feel like I've been playing with fire. I've made a complete idiot of myself!'

'Not from where I'm standing!'

'But Davina you don't understand!'

You see it all started last Wednesday. PW (pre-Wednesday) I was just a lonely being who could only attract the attention of my womanising neighbour (well, him and the office cad who'll shag anything from an admin girl upwards) and spent any spare time usefully feeling sorry for myself.

Now let me see, where did it all go wrong?

The day started with some sort of moral purpose; I can remember thinking I finally had time to go through my emails and clear my in-tray mainly by filing paper in the bin. I soldiered purposefully on, taking action, deleting, moving emails as if I'd just had 10 hours with a life coach on time management for people who are going places. The hours ticked past, only 15 times did I get distracted and peer glumly at the FTSEurofirst 300 index as it continued to enjoy a downhill run. It was like watching Ski-Sunday with a hangover.

So, quite a productive day, really, until six 'o' clock when most self-respecting City dwellers are on their way home to their spouses and I was thinking about heading straight to C&B but decided to give the FTSEuro one more chance. That was when I got a call from reception. I picked up the phone, still staring in disbelief at the screen because I just refuse to take in bad news, and heard this voice say quite calmly:

'Monsieur Éduardo Devereux in reception.'

'Who? What? *In reception*? For who?'

'For you Chloe dear and if I were you I'd get yourself down her rather sharply or I might do something I regret involving throwing myself at him!'

'Geraldine! He can't hear you can he?'

'Chloe, darling he's in the gents preening himself for your loveliness.'

How on earth does she know about our night of madness? Surely it hasn't become gossip round here.

'What are you talking about?'

'Only joking. Anyway, I take it you are coming down?' Then she whispered, 'He's just emerged. My best guess would be suit, Armani; aftershave, Givenchy; Feet, size 15.' She put the phone down. I tried to put my phone down but my hand was trembling. I remained at my desk waiting for a wave of calm to come over me. It didn't. What on earth was he doing on this side of the channel? Why didn't he warn me he was coming? Why on earth did I choose a blouse this morning which reveals too much cleavage and gives the wrong impression to anyone I might have had a one night stand with? Why oh why did I use too much smooth and sleek conditioner in the shower so my hair looks like it's been straightened and coated in olive oil? I distinctly remember that I nearly opted for the total volume which was so readily to hand. I considered getting Davina to phone Geraldine to explain that I'd been taken ill and was leaving by the back exit by ambulance. But actually the bottom line was that knowing that he, as in chiselled features, Greek God, was standing in reception waiting for me turned me into some flimsy piece of metal heading straight for a crash landing into the nearest magnet. Éduardo Devereux. I stood up and immediately my knees buckled but after the first few steps I managed to walk reasonably well. By the time I'd reached reception in the lift I'd given myself a lecture on the morals of relationships with married men which puts E.D. of course completely out of bounds and had decided that this would clearly be a working meeting where professionalism would rule.

'Éduardo, how good to see you! Just passing were you?'

'You must be joking. How does one just pass this island? I came here especially to see you.'

My laugh was ridiculously loud and echoed to the top of the atrium. Thank goodness most people had gone home. But still he continued,

'The fact is that I missed you.'

My knees almost went again, the lift lecture went out of the window and I just wanted to melt.

'Well, it's good to see you.' That was an attempt to bring things down to a level of normality. One I might be able to cope with.

'I've booked a table at the Ivy for dinner; it would be lovely if you could join me.'

The Ivy? For dinner? What is going on? I've heard even Kirsty Young struggles to get a table there these days. I did, I promise you, seriously consider turning him down; I mean I really don't need this and with Jilly Cooper's 'Wicked' now in paperback it would be so much safer to just go home and hole up for the night.

'Dinner at the Ivy? Oh well that sounds like fun. I suppose I don't have too much planned for this evening.'

'Bien! Tres bien! Shall we go?'

'Oh I have to pop back upstairs to finish off but I won't be too long.'

And I was only 20 minutes. Luckily Davina keeps a stash of facial wipes, moisturisers, make-up, talcum powder, perfume (Christian Dior, but I was desperate) spare stockings, tampons and extra sensitive condoms in the bottom of her filing cabinet. All eventualities covered off. And before Eduardo could think 'she must be closing a deal' I was back down in reception thinking three pre-dinner cocktails and I'll stop worrying about, well, anything at all.

It's funny isn't it? Anticipation is everything.

Of course by Thursday 6pm Davina was dragging me down to C&B for a recounting of the evening in minutiae, just when I want to go home and watch 15 episodes of ER.
'Darling! I need detail!'
She looked at me and realised the tale was not of lust but more of confusion.
'Sorry darling I'll shut up. Now drink that Chabbers and tell me why a night with a charming, handsome French man hasn't put a smile on your face.'
I still didn't particularly want to talk about it.
'You alright darling?'
That was it. That was what I needed to hear.
'Of course I'm alright. Just a little jaded.'
'Right. Would you prefer to go somewhere else?'
'Davina, darling, you've just spent thirty quid on a superb bottle of my favourite; we're staying right here.'
'As you wish.' She paused for as long as dear Davina can before she said, 'You know you don't have to tell me a thing.'
So I told her.
'It was fun. The food was fantastic. We laughed and he's really very good company.'
'That sounds terrible.'
'No, no. I mean it. It was a great evening.'
'The last time I had a *great* evening,' Davina re-filled our glasses, 'I had three girlfriends round to eat pizza in front of the first series of Desperate Housewives!'
'I'm not sure why but..'

'You didn't shag! Such restraint! Oh, if you could bottle that!'

I laughed. Davina is so straightforward when it comes to sex. But still I knew she'd understand.

'It was weird really but at some point towards the end of the evening I just knew I'd be happily on the last train home to Lodge Lane.'

'What happened?'

'Nothing really. Just a certainty in my mind that I don't want to be anyone's mistress.'

'Good for you!'

'Thanks.'

There was this amiable silence between us and I felt quite relieved. We sipped our wine, Davina topped up our glasses; we both noticed a few men gazing across at us but didn't care. And then she said,

'It's Alex isn't it?'

The next day I was back sat at my desk staring at the screen not noticing anything. But then slowly I focussed and realised the struggling graph for the Green European Fund had finally managed a turn in the right direction. It looked a bit like a small upturned boat that happened to be lying in a valley. I'd just about made the deadline that Robin had given N.V. of turning it around in a week.

I'd actually made a couple of changes that Alex suggested that night at the lake and much to my relief it was working. So I thought I might as well email him with the good news. I found the last email he'd sent to me, so that I could just hit the reply button and re-read it. It said:

Dear Chloe,

I enjoyed Saturday evening immensely. I can only hope that you did too.'

Alex

Is it me or is that a bit cryptic? *I can only hope that you did too.* I could almost imagine he was falling for me. But hang on a minute. This is Alex MK we're talking about here; womaniser supreme. I really must keep these fantastical notions in check. Eventually I thought what the heck and hit the reply button.

Alex,

Yes it was fun, wasn't it? Just wanted to say thanks for the fund advice which is already having an impact. Hope all's well.

Chloe

I felt a bit mean hitting the send button. It really was rather good; the advice I mean. And the evening out wasn't bad either. Maybe I should reciprocate in some way. No, that would be silly.

Becky

Derek turns out to be OK. I mean obviously he's a useless husband with his wife leaving him and his house is a right old mess. Yeah, we've been allowed in now that we're doing his garden for him, well, in the kitchen and to use the loo. That's enough to give you the general idea. Clutter everywhere, empty ready meal packets piling up, a home brew kit never opened and the loo could definitely benefit from a woman's touch. But what surprised me about dozy Derek is that he reads a posh paper; The Guardian, it is; seems to get it every day. They're piling up in the corner of the kitchen. Now if I had to guess what his daily was I'd put money on The Sun or The Mirror. Makes you think. Maybe there's more to this man than meets the eye. I saw a framed photo the other day of the happy couple. Well they were happy on their wedding day, that is. She looks like she might be a teacher or a nurse maybe; somethin' sensible anyway. Her wedding dress looks like it's strangling her round the neck. No cleavage on show here. She's got Virginia bride written all over her face. No wonder he doesn't get the Sun. Probably thinks he'll end up down below come juggling day.

    It's been back braking stuff doing the garden. To try and turn a mound of mud into something that might save a marriage; well, it's bloody hard work. Alex has been brilliant. He's surprised me actually. You'd think someone from his kinda world would not want to get involved in digging and movin' earth but he's really got stuck in.
    'But Becky, I can't have you doing all the manual work. We're a team and well, I know you're a feisty girl but this is man's work.'
    'Hey I'm not scared of a spade and a bit of hard graft.' But actually even though I consider myself to be pretty strong I was quite chuffed that he thinks I'm a feisty girl and that he

wants to save me from some of the blisters I was bound to get. I suppose he actually cares a bit and you know that gets me every time. I mean a man who gives a damn?

But as I watched him it was like it took over him and he couldn't stop and he just kept going as if he didn't have a clue what was going on around him. I began to think there must be more to all this. It was like he was attacking the mound as if it was something dreadful in his life. The sweat started pouring off him and he was out of breath but still he kept digging.

'Stop! Stop just for a minute!' I shouted. I couldn't help myself.

At first I thought he hadn't heard me 'cos he kept going.

'Alex you mental or what? Stop!'

He looked up at me. Finally he stopped. And he looked around and it was as if it was a complete surprise to him that the mound wasn't there anymore. He looked confused. I walked up to him. I mean I didn't really think about it but it just seemed like the right thing to do. I know he always has a handkerchief in his trouser pocket and so I pulled it out and handed it to him so he could wipe his face. He did wipe it and put the hanky back but without a word and I thought that was weird. And then at last he said, all calm,

'What am I going to do Becky? What am I going to do about Chloe? I mean how am I going to convince her that what I feel for her is genuine?'

Well, this is all news to me. But I must admit it explains a lot. I mean when I first met him I thought he was a bit strange in a la de da kinda way but you always knew what you were going to get. But just recently he's been up and down, moody one minute, cheerful the next. It's like he's on another planet and then suddenly realises what's goin' on so he's normal again.

So he fancies Chloe. Well I suppose she's his type being a bit of a high flyer and havin' a bit of money. She is very pretty too. And she can afford all those expensive face creams and nice make-up, not to mention recliner clothes from posh shops where they call you Madam and bring things for you to try on like it is in the films.

'Why don't you just tell her?' I said but almost wished I hadn't.

'But how?'

I don't understand and I really can't be bothered to work it out. I've just been tryin' so hard to live the dream, the dream of the Green Machine and this all feels like it's gettin' in the way.

'I don't bloody know! You'll have to work that out!' He looked quite surprised but then I said it. 'And in the meantime, if you don't mind we need to get on with this garden. I mean we don't get paid until it's finished and we 'aint got any other work and we're never goin' to make any bleedin' money if we don't keep goin'!'

I felt a bit bad when I realised what I'd said 'cos it sounded like a right old moan but luckily I got the old Alex back for a bit.

'I'm so sorry Becky. I shouldn't bring my personal problems into this.' Oh so Chloe's a personal problem now is she, I thought but didn't say it. Anyway he went on,

'Really this business is as important to me as I know it is to you. And we will make a go of it, I promise.'

But is it? He doesn't have a kid and a diet of baked beans and have to walk everywhere.

'You know in some ways the Chloe thing means it's even more important for me to make a success of this,' he said. Well, it's a bloody funny way of lookin' at things if you ask me but I suppose that's a good thing.

'You alright Becky?' He looked really bothered when he said that.

'Yeah course,' I wasn't sure if I meant it.

'What do you say, you, me and Jack go out for afternoon tea at Tiffins later? My treat.'

I wanted to say no but the thought of little Jack's face lighting up meant I had to say yes.

'If you insist,' I said and then I was kind of lookin' forward to it really.

Alex

The perfect sound has to be the cork popping out of the bottle followed by the glug of the red wine smothering the bowl of the glass. And that's all I can hear down here in the cellar; it's amazingly quiet. Luckily I've still got a few fruits from my labours before I was extracted from City life and I make the time to come down here to indulge my senses. The trouble is, as they say, in the quiet you find yourself. I like to think you take all the thoughts that have been buzzing around in your mind and sort them out.

We've just completed our first major gardening job. Derek's garden is now fit for a princess or at least an estranged wife. I was so proud when we'd completed the finishing touches. Becky installed a stone water feature and picked out some lovely planting.

'Low maintenance,' she told Derek as she looked straight at him. I must say his appearance definitely inspired a need for limited effort in all things. I noticed Becky just taking a moment to stand back and stare and I found myself going to stand next to her.

'Good job, Becky. Well done.'

'Team effort; we work well together don't we?'

I only had to smile and she smiled back. Derek offered one last cup of his rather weak tea and I wasn't going to accept but the little woman beat me to it.

'Oh OK then, one last cup.'

We celebrated in Tiffins, with Jack of course. Chocolate cake all round and rather good it was too. I've never really noticed before but Jack's got enormous blue eyes. He stared at me as he tried to get too much cake in his mouth and grinned to reveal chocolate cream all over his teeth. Far from being horrified it actually made me laugh and I thought he's not a bad little chap. Becky insisted that the cost of the tea came out of the company funds.

'You're not paying. This is to come out of the business.' We both looked at her son and quickly averted our eyes.

'Of course,' I said to keep things simple but I was thinking how it might be about a tenner which was nothing really but to Becky it was an extravagance.

'Where next?' she said brightly, full of hope, no doubt, that the next job would start the following day.

'To be honest I've been so wrapped up with Derek's little piece of England I haven't got anything lined up. No bites from the newsagent's ad.' I felt really bad but then she said,

'Silly me. It's not just down to you. I should be doing my bit. But what do we do? I just wouldn't know where to start.'

'We could get some leaflets printed up and put them through doors.'

'Brilliant idea.'

And so at least we hatched a plan.
I haven't seen Chloe for a couple of weeks now. Each time I wander up into the village I think that maybe I'll bump into her and then I wonder what I'll say. But it hasn't happened so it doesn't matter. The other day I wandered into The Green Antiques more out of curiosity than an intention to buy anything, only to be confronted with a startled Sheila.

'Alex, what are you doing here?'
Goodness knows what sort of answer that deserved but then the owner stepped in,

'Excuse my mother, David Harrington, new owner at you service,' he shook my hand and his eyes lit up. I wondered if he thought maybe I had a lot of money and I was planning to spend it in his shop.

'Alex Minter-Kemp, good to meet you.'

It was then that a man appeared from the back, he looked like he was walking straight off the set of Brideshead

Revisited after a scene with Jeremy Irons, just the teddy bear missing.

'David, sweetie pie, who have we *here*?'

They were now both staring at me and I must admit I felt a little uncomfortable. Sheila looked pale and this was clearly her son and his gay lover. Surely she knew about it. I was just inventing an exit strategy when I got a second introduction.

'Nigel Price, fabulous to meet you.' Luckily he settled for shaking my hand too and I must admit I started to see the funny side. Sheila has certainly kept this skeleton locked in the closet.

'Well this is a surprise; such a welcome addition to the village.' I said breezily but then felt a little bad as Sheila looked like she needed a stiff drink and might keel over at any moment. David ignored her.

'I'm glad you think so. Actually we're holding a little drinks party to launch the new shop; Thursday 6pm. You simply must come!'

'Right, I'll bear that in mind.' I said and was turning to leave when David said.

'What's your line of business Alex? Something in the City I expect?'

'Oh no, used to be. These days I run a gardening business with my neighbour Becky.' It felt strange saying it but somehow good.

'Well we know where to come if we need some muscle action in the garden then,' Nigel joked or at least I hope he was joking. At this point I simply had to rescue Sheila.

'Sheila, I'm popping into The Grasshopper on the way home, care to join me?'

'Oh, no, I mean yes. Yes! Wonderful.'

'Good.' I managed a smile as I left the two lovers looking bemused.

With two brandies in front of us, I said, 'It's OK Sheila. It's really OK. These days anything goes. Good for your son, I mean running his own business. Good for him.' She downed the brandy in one.

'Thanks Alex. You don't know what that means to me.' The colour had returned to her cheeks and she simply said, 'One for the road?'

Sheila

George hasn't spoken to me for five days. Just because I didn't tell him about David moving into the village it's my fault. My fault that he's not a raving heterosexual, happily married with 2.4 children. My fault he can't be gay in another county at least; ideally another country!

'Oh, yes, David's abroad,' we'd say to anyone who enquired, 'rather a successful businessman.' Why would there be any need to mention his sexuality or lack of a female partner?

George spends more time than ever in the shed. I've not even bothered to look but I wouldn't be surprised if he's built an extension at the back and added on a kitchen. He certainly doesn't want much in the way of meals from me. He's taken to walking pointedly out of the house at 6pm, the time I used to be required to serve up dinner. I can only assume he dines in the pub. It's left me with a strange kind of freedom I'm not used to. Liberated from the shackles of having to please; being able to decide what *I* want, *when* I want it. Last night I ate paella listening to Jose Carreras, 'Love songs from Spain' on full blast. It felt delicious. By the sound of the rather loud and agitated knock at the door, Becky must have been there for a while before I heard her. When I opened the door she was almost laughing.

'Becky, how are you?'

'Hello Sheila, everything OK?' she said still smiling.

'Yes everything's just wonderful.'

'Oh good, it's just you don't normally hear much from your place and I just wondered what was going on with the posh music. You and George OK?'

'I'm marvellous. George is out.'

'Oh I see, while the cat's away.'

'Something like that,' I said not feeling the need to explain.

'Well, as long as you're OK?'

'Sorry, I'll turn it down a bit. But silly me, why don't you come in!' George has never liked spontaneous visits from neighbours especially in the evenings. 'Yes, come in for a glass of wine!'

She looked at me oddly and said, 'well I'm tempted but I have to get back to little Jack.'

'Oh bring him with you; he's good as gold; don't worry about that!'

'Oh, OK. Give me a few minutes then.'

After the first glass of wine, or was it the second, it just all came out, all the stuff about David. But not in a way that it was some tragic tale, just telling Becky what was what as if it's all perfectly normal. And that's how it feels right now.

'Oh I think I've seen him. Is he the one with blond hair?'

'That's the one! His gay lover, Nigel, is the dark one.'

'Well they seem very happy. I wish I owned an antique shop.'

'But you've got a gardening business with Alex! Lucky you! He's rather nice, that Alex don't you think?'

'Blimey you don't fancy him do you Sheila?'

'Not much point really; he'd never be interested in me!' we both laughed at that and it felt good.

'He's a good bloke actually; he can be quite surprising, but way too la de da for me. I'd have to have those electrificution lessons!'

I didn't bother to correct her. I think it's lovely that she gets the odd word wrong. Why does everyone have to follow the rules; I've had enough of rules!

'Actually, I can let you into a secret,' she said leaning over as if she didn't want Jack to hear, 'he fancies Chloe. Well actually I think he's pretty stuck on her. He seems quite disturbed at times.'

'That's no good! Love should be a wonderful thing! Something to excite and thrill you! Not disturb you!'

'Oh, Sheila, I'm definitely seeing another side of you tonight. And somehow I don't think it's just the wine.'

I noticed the bottle was empty and did something I don't think I've ever done before; I opened another. It was white and it hadn't been in the fridge but I thought what the heck.

'You know, I think you're right. I feel different; I feel good! Anyway, tell me more about Alex and Chloe. I want the gossip. That's what my life lacks, gossip!'

She laughed, 'Well I'm not sure that anything much has happened. I mean he just got all worked up the other day when we was digging Derek's garden and he suddenly says, "How am I going to convince her of my feelings." It was like a line in some Shakespeare play.'

'Goodness, he has got it bad. So what about her? I mean she's been on her own a while, hasn't she?'

'Search me.'

'Maybe we should bring them together!'

'Oh I don't know. I suppose it would be alright. I just want the Green Machine to start working first.'

Becky looked quite troubled then. Even though I'd had quite a lot to drink I could tell there was a weight on her mind.

'Is it not going well?'

'Well we have our moments but we're not doing any marketing. That's what Alex says.'

'Do you have any business cards?'

'No, I don't think so.'

'I'll get you some printed. What is it, The Green Machine?' I wrote it down. I found the piece of paper this morning.

'But how will you do that?'

'Don't you worry. I've got a bit put by. And when they're printed I'll hand them out to everyone! My dog walking clients are just the type for you – too busy to walk their dogs; they must be too busy to do their gardens.'

'That's a good point.'

'Then there's choir. More of a tight bunch but you never know.'

She laughed and I thought what good company she'd turned out to be and how we should do this more often. It felt so good being able to help. Becky's face lit up and when she was going I said, 'And I'll look after Jack any time you like.' And she hugged me.

George gave me a very strange look when he got back from the pub as he passed through the house and into the shed. I made myself a cup of tea and took it up to the spare room where I sleep now. I giggled myself to sleep and I actually felt quite liberated, but of course I'm not.

Becky

I still can't talk very well because the blow to the side of my face got the corner of my mouth. It feels like I'm bruised all over; I feel sore if I try to move, but still, I do. Because I won't let him win. He somehow got round the back and into the garden. A few days ago it was, now. It was a lovely evening and Jack was in bed so I was just sitting out thinking how warm it was even though it was dark and the pink rose tree had a wonderful smell.

'Think you're bloody Lady Muck now do you?' he came up behind me. God knows how he got in without me even hearing him.

'Eddie! What are you doing here?'

'Just checking up on my wife,' he said and he was really angry even though I hadn't done anything and of course I'm not his wife anymore.

'What do you want Eddie?' My voice was trembling and that really annoyed me because of course he knew I was scared.

'Think you can hide from me do you?' I was supposed to be in a safe place.

'I'm just getting on with my life.' I thought of Jack and prayed he wouldn't try to see him.

'Micky told me see. He knows you're working for that gardening chap now.' Of course I'm not working for Alex but there was no point in even mentioning that.

'Posh neighbourhood hey? You wound the social up good and proper didn't you?'

'No. No I was entitled. They said. Anyway it's just a small place.'

'I suppose having a kid helps you plead your case and of course all the lies you fed them about me.'

'No, no they just found this place for me to live. That's all.'

'Well it's not been so great for me!'

'I'm sorry Eddie.'

'How bloody sorry?'

And that was it. It was no good because I'm not sorry at all and I couldn't lie any more than I had already. I just had to take it. It makes me so angry just thinking about it. Angry. Upset. Useless. How he can turn up and beat me up just because he's bigger and stronger than me?

After he'd gone I just lay on the ground for ages; I don't know if I went out completely or not. I was trying desperately hard not to because I was so worried about little Jack and I just wanted to go up to his room and hold him. I didn't even know if Eddie had taken him or not. It took ages but I did manage to get up there. I was shakin' all over even though I knew I'd locked all the doors and anyway he was unlikely to come back; at least not tonight. Seeing Jack lying there in his little bed was such a relief but I just burst out crying. I couldn't help it. Goodness knows how and I picked him up and took him into my bed. I just lay there clinging on to him, my tears wetting the pillow until I went to sleep. Luckily he didn't wake.

In the morning he woke me clawing at my face.

'Mummy, mummy is red.'

'Yes, my brave boy, mummy is hurt.' I wondered for a minute whether I'd be able to move. It felt like my whole body had seized up over night. But Jack looked so sad I couldn't bear it. 'We'll stay here together today; just you and me, and you can help Mummy get better.'

As I swung my legs to the floor the blood rushed through the soreness creating a dreadful pain but I couldn't let my baby know how bad it was.

We stayed in all day. There were several knocks at the door which I just ignored. I thought maybe it was Alex about a job or Sheila about the business cards. Whatever, I couldn't let anyone see me in this state. Then Alex rang my mobile and I decided to answer otherwise he might come round again.

'Becky you sound different, what's wrong?'

I made a massive effort to sound normal and said, 'Would you believe, just an accident; tryin' to reach a tin of baked beans from the top shelf and they fell on my mouth.'

'Oh, Becky can I do anything to help? Take you to casualty maybe?'

'Oh no thanks, I'll be alright in a couple of days.'

'But are you sure, it's no trouble.'

'I've got to go, it's Jack you see.'

'But Becky, why don't I..'

I cut him off. I felt bad but I just couldn't face anyone.

But then, the next day I got too near the lounge window, picking something up for Jack, and there was Sheila staring in at me. She looked really worried.

'Oh Becky, Becky darling, you must let me in.'

Well, what else could I do? Stick to the baked beans story but pretend there were loads of them falling down on me? Not bloody likely. I've only ever got a couple of tins. I opened the door and I just couldn't help it; I burst out crying. Sheila hugged me and told me everything would be OK now and I thought that was a really good thing to say because quite frankly I couldn't carry on if I thought it was going to be anything but alright. She sat me on the sofa, gave Jack a toy to play with and made us both a cup of tea. We sipped in silence for a while; she didn't ask any questions and then I decided I was ready to tell her.

'It was Eddie. We were married and he beat me up so they moved me here. They called it a safe place.'

'Oh, Becky, darling, you poor thing.'

'It was the other evening, he just appeared from nowhere. He wanted me and of course I can't do that so he beat me up.'

Now Sheila had a tear in her eye.

'Why on earth didn't you let me know?'

'Stupid thing is I feel ashamed. It's his bloody fault, I know, but I'm the one who ends hidin' stuff. I just want things to go back to normal. I'm more worried about Jack than anything else.'

'Of course you are. He seems OK.'

'Yeah, he's brilliant.'

'How bad is it?' she asked.

'I'm covered in cuts and bruises. It hurts to walk but I'm managing.'

She didn't say anything for a while although I think she wanted to say a lot.

'You're very brave, Becky.' And she smiled and I managed to smile back, well sort of crooked probably.

'It's all part of me. Being Becky. There's no easy rides. I just get on with it.'

And then she surprised me more than ever before.

'I'm moving in, for a while anyway. Until you're better and until we come up with a plan to make sure this doesn't happen again.'

The funny thing was, I was really pleased. I've never been so scared in my life. I'm just waiting for him to come back. I won't even let Jack play in the garden.

'But what about George, you can't just leave him.'

'Oh, he probably won't even notice. I'm already sleeping in the spare room.'

'Oh Sheila, I'm sorry to hear that.'

'Oh don't be. I'm quite enjoying it. No snoring to put up with and I can read in the middle of the night if I fancy it!'

She sounded almost pleased about the situation and I wondered what was going on but I decided she'll tell me if she wanted to.

'But are you sure, about moving in here, I mean?'

'Very sure,' she said and yes, you've guessed it; it made me cry again.

And so she's here. Well not at the moment she's doing her dog walking but I have her mobile number just in case and I've got the doors locked. She's been looking after me like a mum and it's ever so nice because my mum died when I was little and I've never known my dad. She sleeps in Jack's room and he's in with me which is fine except he accidentally kicks me in the night sometimes. She makes me take paracetamol every four hours and she gave me some funny herbs to take last night to make me sleep. And they worked. She does all the shopping and won't let me pay for it and she cooks me and Jack really lovely meals; we haven't had baked beans once. She says it's to help me get better.

Last night she even opened a bottle of wine after Jack had gone to bed and after a glass I felt quite woozy and so when she said,

'So what are we going to do to stop him?' I felt like I was ready.

'I wish they'd lock him up and throw away the key but you know that ain't ever gonna happen.'

'Do you have a social worker?'

'Yeah, course I do, Josie her name is. Single mum with violent ex, bound to aren't I? One of the privileged, that's what I've always thought.'

Sheila looked sad but then she seemed to shake herself out of it. 'Shall we give her a call tomorrow?'

'Yeah, but I don't want to move from here. I've just got to know you all and even Alex turns out to be a good bloke and all me dreams in The Green Machine. I just can't leave it all behind. I just want to stay here now.'

She topped up both our glasses and handed mine back to me so I didn't have to move too much.

'Becky, I promise you, whatever happens, you won't have to move.'

You know Sheila, she's bloody brilliant!

Chloe

David, my ex, called the other day. It's been just over three years since we split. The divorce went through easily as we were in agreement. Well, at least I agreed he was a prat for marrying me in the first place when I'd made it clear I didn't want children.

'But darling I thought you'd change your mind once we were together properly,' he'd argued with that gentle tone that irritates me to death now. 'You with a ring on your finger living in marital bliss; I thought the need for a successful career would subside.'

As if his teacher's salary was going to keep us in the life we'd become accustomed to if I gave up work! I suppose he was ready to settle for less. Anyway, he was phoning about the antique chest we had bought together when we were setting up home.

'I was just wondering if you still use it?'

What a ridiculous question! As if you buy a fine-looking antique to 'use it'. OK I might store things in it but essentially it is a piece of furniture to be admired.

'Well I still have it, if that's what you mean?'

'It's just that we bought it originally to store things in, for when we were married, didn't we?'

'No! Well, I didn't.'

'Oh. Well do you still want it?'

'Yes, I bloody do! It was part of the divorce settlement and I'm keeping it!'

I remembered the dividing of the material possessions well; David always opting for practicality over beauty. For the chest he probably got a hoover and a toaster.

'Oh,' he said and went quiet for a moment but not long enough.

'Have you met someone?' What was that supposed to mean? And what on earth has that got to do with an antique chest! Is this a sudden change of subject? Has he suddenly decided to get jealous?

'No! I mean yes! But nothing serious.' What did I mean? I was hardly sure myself. Anyway it's none of his business.

'Oh, I see.' What did he see?

'The thing is,' he continued and I just knew I wasn't going to like what came next. All through our marriage, whenever he said 'the thing is', disaster struck.

'I have.' I have?

'You've what?'

'I've met someone.' He said it sheepishly as if he was slightly worried how I might react. And the awful thing was I was jealous in a strange sort of way. Not because he's met someone but because I haven't!

'So you've met someone. Great!' That couldn't have sounded more sarcastic.

'I'm sorry Chloe, but we are divorced now.' What a wonderful statement of the obvious. Now I really hated him.

'David, no need to be sorry. It's fine. I'm just wondering why you bothered to phone me up to tell me. After all, I really don't give a shit.'

'Ah well, the thing is...' Oh my God, twice in the same phone call. How was I going to cope? I braced myself for something truly dreadful but sadly he surpassed even my worst fears.

'The thing is, Chloe, Sam and I are getting married and we'd like the antique chest as a sort of bottom drawer kind of thing. When I told her about it she said it sounded perfect.'

Words failed me. In fact at that moment I felt that life had failed me. I did the only thing I was physically capable of and placed the receiver back in its cradle. I tried to drop my shoulders and took a few deep breaths. Of course he rang straight back and I decided the answer machine would be able to cope better than me.

'Chloe, you there? I think we got cut off. Pick up will you, Chloe? I'm sorry but the thing is, Sam's expecting and so we want to get married fairly quickly. She doesn't want it to show on the wedding photos. And so I mentioned the chest and she said she would really like it. I thought you'd understand. I mean do you really need it?' He rambled on until the long bleep sounded, indicating even the answer machine had had enough. I poured myself a glass of wine and sat in the garden.

I must have been staring at the beautifully cut lawn, the tidy beds and the pretty flowers for some time but could only see David's face as he grinned at me when I walked up the aisle. Even then I wondered, is this it? But the approving grins of the congregation, the endless congratulation and good wishes, the pile of presents containing every gadget known to man all confirmed I was doing the right thing.

It was only then I noticed the roses bordering the top edge of the lawn, a delicate pale pink. They were beautiful! And the scent! But I certainly haven't planted them! I got closer, peered at them and touched them to make sure they were real. The daffodils that were more familiar, now dead, had been neatly tied up and sat behind the marvellous display of pink. There's definitely something strange going on here. Then I remembered Becky. Sheila had told me. So I got the kitchen scissors and cut half a dozen of the loveliest stems and then some green foliage to complement them. Inside I found a glass vase and as I took it out the cupboard I remembered David's face as he opted for an electrical knife sharpener in retaliation for the vase.

I was pleased with the display and took it straight round to Becky's. Sheila answered the door looking like a woman in residence with her apron on.

'Oh, hi Sheila, just wondering if Becky's up to visitors now?'

'Just hang on a minute.'

She was soon back at the door. 'Yes, come in Chloe.'

I knew it was bad from what Sheila had said but seeing Becky's small frame and pale skin battered and bruised made me swallow hard and fight back a tear.

'Becky, darling, how are you?'

'Oh, you know, not so bad.'

I hugged her gently and kissed her right cheek avoiding the damage on the left.

'I bought these. Your garden's full of lovely flowers, I know, but I just wanted to bring something.'

'Ah the pink roses. Thank you, they're lovely.' I put them on the hearth and Sheila quickly moved them to a shelf.

'It's Jack see. Has his little hands on everything,' Becky explained.

'Sorry.'

'Don't be silly. Sit down for a bit. This is funny isn't it? I've never had so many visitors!'

'Tea?' Sheila offered.

'Lovely.' I said, wishing I'd bought a bottle of wine round instead. But then I found myself alone with Becky and wondering what to say to her but I needn't have worried, her spirit certainly wasn't dampened.

'Sheila's been great. She's been lookin' after me. Actually she's even sleeping here.'

'Really? Does that make you feel a bit safer?'

'Oh yeah, I feel much better, especially after dark. That's when it happened see.'

I wanted to ask her about it but I thought she might not want to talk about it.

'Alex says I need better security.'

'Oh!' I struggled to hide my surprise. 'Alex has been round?'

'Oh yes, I'm havin' visitors every day. I feel like the bloody Queen! Her Royal Highness Becky will see you now; do come through to the drawing room!'

We laughed together and I admired her tenacity.

'Did you call the police?'

'Nah. Sheila and I thought about it. The social, the old bill. Trouble is, I know you see, been there done it, got the bleedin' T-shirt. Bottom line is they come in, take over and end up messin' yer life up. You see it's all his word against mine, with no witnesses. And the social workers are even worse! They spend most of the time fillin' forms in. God knows where all these forms end up but I'll tell you one thing they don't do you any bloody good.'

I smiled at her. Such a brave soldier. So savvy in the world of being a single mum with an abusive ex-husband. 'Sounds like you're better off without them.'

'Too bloody right.'

'But you do need help. We can't let this happen again. I'll do anything I can Becky.'

'Oh Chloe, that means ever such a lot to me. Sheila's doing a great job although I know she has to go back to George at some point. Alex has contacted a security locksmith, he's coming round some time tomorrow to do a seizure.'

'Would that be an assessment?'

'That's it. Sorry, I've never had one before.'

'Anyway Alex says we're paying for it out of The Green Machine money. Apparently it's more important that I'm fit and well. I never know how these things work but he said he wasn't listening to any arguments and that was that.'

'The Green Machine?' I had to ask.

'Yeah, Alex and I have set up a gardening business. Obviously we've had a bit of a setback, but Alex is getting a couple more jobs lined up while I'm like this. But I'll be OK soon.'

'That's good.' This was surprising; Alex setting up a gardening business with Becky. I was quite intrigued but she changed the subject.

'Anyway, enough about me, you been jet setting around as usual have you?'

'Oh, yes, a couple of trips but I'm in London mainly.'

'I suppose you've noticed the garden. Oops perhaps I shouldn't have said.'

'Yes, I have actually, is that down to you?'

'Alex mainly. Of course I'm the brains behind it!' she laughed at that.

'But why?'

'Oh Chloe! Don't you know? Alex has got the hots for you!'

'Oh! Well I suppose so. I think he has the hots for lots of women actually.'

'Well he certainly doesn't have them for me,' Becky said.

'Nor me!' Sheila appeared with the tea and I think I blushed.

The three of us sat and chatted. I thought about how different we all were and yet how it's so unimportant in a crisis. I didn't know what I could do to help right then but I hoped I would come up with something. At one point I nearly told them about the phone call with David.

'Actually my ex-husband called earlier.'

'Oh, what did he want?' Becky was interested.

I looked at the bruise on her face and almost felt ashamed. 'Oh, nothing really. Trying to scrounge back an antique chest I ended up with. Nothing important.'

Alex

I've never really bothered with religion. My parents are the sort that turn up for occasions – weddings, funerals, Easter, Christmas - as if they live their lives as devout Christians but forget about it in between. So when Sheila suggested it, I was reluctant to say the least.

'The Sunday morning service isn't bad,' she informed me. 'Only an hour or so of worship and hymns and then everyone moves to the back room for coffee and biscuits.'

'I think I'd feel like a decent drop of Claret at an Asti Spumante party.' Sheila laughed at that thankfully.

'But Alex, you're missing the point.'

'What's that? The good Lord is going to bring divine intervention and improve the fortunes of The Green Machine?'

'No, silly. You'll be able to get to know the locals. Take the coffee bit as a chance to mingle. They're bound to ask you what you do for a living.' She looked at me as if I should finish her sentence.

'Oh I see, I tell them I'm a gardener.'

'Yes! Tell them about The Green Machine.'

'Right. Well it's worth a try. I must get some new clients lined up for when Becky's up to it.'

'Yes, and now you have the business cards to hand out,'

'Yes, thanks for organising that. I shall definitely hand them out at every opportunity.'

She had a concerned look on her face and I could understand why. Since the Becky incident I'd not been on top form or quite as driven to get The Green Machine going as I previously thought. It was just another setback we could do without. But of course coping with adversity is what it's all about. I tell myself there's a prize at the end of it all.

'How is the little lady today?'

'She's definitely on the mend.' Sheila explained. 'I've noticed she moves more easily now and she even came dog walking with me yesterday. Jack's back at playgroup. Yes, things are getting back to normal.'

'I'd better get a move on then,' I said and at last I felt spurred on.

Well I can report that the congregation of St. Peter at Hartfield are not a bad bunch. Although most of them seemed to think I was there to find a wife which would have been fairly tricky amongst them. The sermon was all about turning the other cheek and I thought of Becky and how it was difficult to apply that to her situation. I stumbled my way through the hymns, just attempting the odd longer note; my mother told me I couldn't sing when I was five and I've not bothered to question that ever since. As Sheila promised, watery coffee and anemic looking biscuits were duly served up. A youngish woman – well relatively speaking, probably mid-thirties – pounced first.

'Are you new to the village? I've not seen you here before?' she said with an energy and enthusiasm best kept for other situations in my book.

'Yes, not been here long.' I decided not to reveal my hedonistic behaviour to date before finally succumbing to God.

'Lizzie Wentworth.' She offered a hand.

'Alex Minter-Kemp.' I thought of a hundred crass things to say but luckily she spoke first.

'We're not a bad bunch; quite sociable really. Toby and I do am dram, fabulous fun and he's on the governor's board of the local school where our children go. Do you have children?'

I wondered if she had me down for some sort of sad widower bringing up three boys on my own, not a moment to think for myself.

'No, sadly not.' Why did I say that? I've never wanted children? This church thing was having a strange effect.

'Married?' She asked casually and I wondered if she fancied a fling with me while Toby was on his governing duties.

'No.' That was the answer and there were lots of so called explanations as to why I wasn't, mainly going back to the hedonistic lifestyle but what was it appropriate to say in a church.

'I suppose I just haven't been lucky enough to find the right woman.' As I said that I couldn't help thinking of Chloe, although marrying her seemed a bit drastic. I'm not sure what expression this brought about but it certainly seemed to stir something in Lizzie.

'Such a shame, a man of your age and stature living alone.' The look that accompanied that comment would definitely have a certificate 18 if ever broadcast.

It was then I remembered I was supposed to be talking about gardening and tried the obvious route.

'So how do you keep yourself busy Mrs Wentworth?'

'Oh. Call me Lizzie. Anyway who says I'm always busy?' Her eye twinkled and she got even closer to me. This was clearly a disastrous line of enquiry so I changed tack.

'Good for you, of course my gardening business keeps me very busy.'

'Oh you're a gardener! How wonderful! I'd never of guessed. Those hands look like they belong on the end of a pin stripe suit.'

'Ah well that was a past life. Also I have a partner; we work together.' That seemed to calm her down a bit.

'Excellent,' had a subdued tone and then, 'I suppose I should find my husband.'

Sheila's pep talk kicked in and I decided I had nothing to lose, 'Would you like one of these.' I handed her a business card for The Green Machine.

'Oh, your phone number!' Her eyes widened and her eye lashes flickered. I wasn't sure if I was pleased or terrified.

The next encounter was easier.

'Alex isn't it?'

'Er yes.'

'I'm Linda. Lovely to meet you at last.'

'At last, is it?'

'It's not often we get newcomers to the village; word gets about you see.'

The woman before me was a voluptuous vision of pink and turquoise, her cleavage on splendid display with the strangest furry lime green hand bag thrown across one shoulder.

'How you settling in? Brave of you to come to church on your own!'

'Oh well actually I rather like this little village. Everyone is so friendly.' Sheila would have been proud of me.

'Yes, especially Lizzie Wentworth!' She laughed a loud chortle and I joined in although I wasn't sure if this was wise.

'Don't worry about her. She'll soon calm down. Anyway what brings you to these parts?'

'Ah well. Change of circumstance; left the City and decided to settle in the country and set up a gardening business.' Well that sounded a lot more purposeful than the real course of events.

'Ah, so a change of direction! I like that. Yes, when I look back on my life I see new adventures emerging in every decade.'

'Gosh that sounds exciting!'

'Well truth be told most of it was forced on me; lovers leaving, husbands dying, disastrous finances. Although I can say my spell being self-sufficient up in the Highlands for a couple of years was definitely a whim which left me questioning my own sanity. Still I've dined out on it ever since!' Again she laughed out loud and it was clear the rest of the congregation were used to this dear woman. I liked her honesty and the last thing I wanted to do was start selling the business again but as it happened I needn't of worried.

'So how's it going, this gardening business?'

'Oh, not bad. Could do with a few more regular clients, though.'

'Yeah, they're a tight bunch round here but I do know that quite a few have very large gardens. I'll keep my ears and eyes open for you, Alex.'

'Oh, thanks Linda. That would be splendid. I've got these business cards with the details if they're any use.'

'Perfect! Give them to me and I'll hand them round!' And with that she took the whole lot.

That evening Freddy came over, hauled me out of my cellar and forced me to play squash.

'But I'm not in the mood. I've just drunk a bottle of Claret old boy.'

'All the more reason to thrash round a court for a bit. We can't have you stagnating.'

'Perfect recipe for a headache if you ask me.'

'I'm not. Now get your whites on.'

I drank a couple of litres of water and funnily enough I found the game quite invigorating. Admittedly the ball might as well have been in my head for the first few whacks but after that I succumbed to the fight in me and let rip.

'Bloody hell, old boy, you're winning! What was all that crap about a bottle of Claret?'

I couldn't help smiling. 'I guess there's a lot of frustration in there and I need to let it out.'

After three defeats Freddy got his white handkerchief out and waved it at me. 'My round?'

The lager was cold and sweet and hit the spot.

'You having women problems, Alex, old boy?

'What women?'

'You know that Clarissa one.'

'Chloe!' I corrected him rather loudly.

'Ah, yes, the one you've really fallen for. So what's the score? Given current form I take it you haven't shagged her yet?'

It's my reaction to stuff like that which worries me slightly. I've spent a good deal of my life with the sole aim of shagging every desirable woman I come across but with Chloe it's a whole new ball game. I desire her beautiful mind as well as her body and the word 'shag' just isn't appropriate here.

'No, I've not shagged her,' was all I could be bothered to say.

'Well the sooner the better if you ask me.'

When I was finally shot of Freddy (actually that's not very fair; I was pleased he'd got me out of my brooding state in the end) I checked my phone for messages. The first was what sounded like a genuine enquiry for the Green Machine and made me smile. The second was a text message that read:

Alex, Thursdays at 3 suits me best. 5 Church Rd. Use back gate and will tell all you're my new gardener! Longing Lizzie xxx

There it was; sex offered in true British tradition. I switched my phone off and went to bed.

Becky

Today has been a very sad day. It's really made me think especially as the sun has been shining on the garden and it looks so pretty.

The phone rang about 9.30 this morning. I don't get many calls so I just assumed it was Alex. So sure of meself I was, 'Hello mate.'
'Er, hello. Erm is that Rebecca Wright?'
Me immediate thought was the social. Maybe they got wind of Eddie's visit; maybe they wanted to move me.
'Who's askin?'
'My name is Doreen Mapleton. I'm a solicitor.'
Blimey, I thought, surely they haven't caught the bugger.
'This is about Eddie isn't it?
'No, it's not about Eddie. Please madam, can I establish that you are indeed Rebecca Wright?'
'What's it about then?'
'I really do need to know who you are before I can tell you that.'
I was really scared by now but it was no good. 'Yes, I am. Becky actually. No one ever calls me Rebecca.'
'I'm sorry Becky.' Why was she being nice now?
'Are you sitting down?' she asked and I thought this is going to be bad news 'cos they never ask you that if it's good. I wasn't but I perched on the arm of the sofa. 'OK ready now.'
'Becky, I'm really sorry to have to tell you that Edith Robinson has passed away.'
'Nah, don't be silly, not Mrs R. She's gotta live forever. I mean she's always been good to me and her garden well it's just bloody amazing and...'
'You were obviously very close.'
'She's really gone, hasn't she?'

'I'm afraid so Becky.'

I suddenly felt very scared, and hopeless 'cos she's gone and there's nothing I can do about it. Life suddenly seemed so precious.

'She was 82, so she had a long and I'm sure happy life.' That's what she said. That's what they all say if they're old when they die. Like it's OK. I always thought 82 was quite young and she'd live to a 100 at least.

'The funeral is on Wednesday at 2 'o clock and it is at the church in her village, Halstead.'

'Will it be alright if I go?'

'Of course it will.'

'I don't think I'll truly believe it unless I see it with me own eyes.'

There was a long pause and I was wondering why she wasn't saying goodbye.

'Is that it then? I suppose that's why you rang?'

'Well actually Becky, I'm going to need to talk to you at some point.'

'What me?'

'Yes, I was wondering if I could have a word after the funeral?'

'What about?'

'It's about Edie's estate.'

'What you mean her garden and everything?'

'Well, yes.'

'Me and Alex will still do the garden if that's what you're worried about?'

'No, Becky. I do need to talk to you face to face.'

I dragged myself round to Alex's place and luckily he was in.

'Hello Becky, you alright?'

'No, Alex I'm not. Mrs R is dead. What am I going to do?'

'Oh Becky, that's very sad, I'm so sorry.'
I knew he'd make me feel better, having met her and everything. He made some tea and we sat in his garden and talked about how great she was. He said about how life is so short and we all have to make the most of it.

'It makes me glad that we set up the Green Machine, Becky. It feels like we're doing something worthwhile. Edie would be proud of us.'

And you know although that made me cry it also made me happy in a funny kinda way.

Sheila

George has changed the locks. I can't get in. I can't get in to my own home. I can see the peace lily, my favourite plant as it happens, on the window sill but I can't touch it, water it or take care of it. I thought about the soft pillows on my bed. Silly really but the ones at Becky's aren't as comfortable. I thought about my teapot. I've had it for nearly twenty years. But it's all out of reach now that I'm locked out. I didn't really know what to do. I could of gone straight back next door but I know that's just temporary and I can't impose for too long. Although I do know Becky appreciates me being there right now. Anyway I walked up the road and into this café and ordered a cup of tea, the woman said she'd bring it over and smiled.

'You OK?,' she asked as if maybe I wasn't.

'Oh yes. Well I think so.' I don't normally say things like that to people I don't know. I sat outside on one of the little tables on the street and watched the village going about its business. They don't look like they've just been locked out. For them it's just a normal day.

The funny thing is, as I tried to turn the key I was almost pleased it didn't go in. Maybe because it's a sign from George; finally a reaction. Still no words but he has spoken. He doesn't want me there. Or, he's so upset with me he wants to hurt me back.

'Do you take sugar?' the woman put a small tray in front of me with a teapot and a cup and saucer and a small jug of milk.

'No,' I replied but actually at that moment I wasn't sure whether I did or not.

She looked at me as if she was about to say something but then thought better of it and went back inside.

Mrs Grimshaw from choir walked up the street and went into the Chemists, probably to get her husband's prescription.

He has high blood pressure. She didn't notice me. I don't think her eye sight is all that good. The other day at rehearsal she started singing Jerusalem whilst the rest of us were singing Abide With Me.

Geoffrey, the butcher, stood outside his shop and watched while one of his elderly customers crossed the road. She landed safely and waved. He waved back before returning to his counter. Now that's what I call service. I go in there once a week; George really likes the lamb chops. Well, I used to.

There were a few youths outside the Co-op, hands in pockets hoods up on this lovely sunny day. They think they've got nothing better to do than hang around. I feel sad for them but there's nothing I can do.

My cup was empty but I could squeeze another half cup out of the pot. I put the milk in and remembered that I stopped taking sugar about fifteen years ago. George stopped at the same time to make it easier. We were both putting on a bit of weight so we decided to cut back a bit. It worked for me. I'm not sure it worked for George. Maybe he's got a secret supply of sugar stashed in his shed. Goodness knows what's in there. The last time I took a peep it looked like organized chaos. Lots of useless objects and a few useful ones all with their place, even if that place was in a neat pile. It looked quite cosy, quite homely. It was almost as if he'd moved out and left me even then.

A man appeared in a silver sports car, Mercedes, I think. The roof was down and I could see he was a handsome chap, the colour of his hair matching his car. When he climbed out I could see he was tall and it was quite surprising that he fitted in there. He was very smartly dressed in a pin stripe suit and I wondered what he was doing in Hartfield. He walked straight into the bank. The one where I deposit my earnings from my dog walking each week. And then it occurred to me that I've never looked to see how much is in there and I've been dog walking for, well it must be three months now. Probably not enough for a sports car!

The tea was definitely all gone. They weren't exactly busy in the café and I don't suppose they minded me just sitting there but I thought maybe it's time to move on.

I had to walk past The Green Antiques to get to the church but David didn't see me. But when I got to the big oak doors I decided it was too risky as I might bump into the vicar. I wasn't in the mood for a heart to heart with him of all people. I don't suppose he encourages marriage breakdown. Is that really what this is?

The second time I walked past David's shop he spotted me.

'Hi Mum, how's it going?' He kissed me on the cheek.

'Hi David, how are you?'

'Come in. I'll make you a cup of tea.'

'Oh yes, that would be lovely.' Of course I didn't want more tea. The shop looked impressive; they must have done a lot of work and bought in quite a bit of new stock. They've started selling those humorous greetings cards. I read a couple and laughed but I didn't really find them funny.

'Mum, what's happening? You don't look like your normal self?'

'Don't I? I've been looking after Becky.'

'Who's Becky?'

'She's my neighbour. Her ex beat her up.'

'Oh nasty. Is she OK?'

'Yes, she's very brave and healing too.' I managed a smile.

A customer wanted to pay for a cutlery service. David was full of banter and the customer left laughing. He does his job well. He looked at me.

'So Mum, what's going on?' I don't know, one minute I look a bit peaky and the next there's something going on. Does my face really reveal so much? I thought of lots of evasive answers, even pretended to be interested in an old colander. But it was no good. I've never been able to hide the truth from David.

'Your father has had the locks changed on the house. I'm locked out.'

'What? Why would he do that?'

'Well I suppose I did sort of leave him.'

'You've left him?'

'Not exactly. I moved in with Becky to look after her.

'Does he know that?'

'He's not speaking to me. Hasn't been for some time.'

'Since when?' I could see it dawning on his face and he said it before I could make up some excuse.

'Since *I* moved in to the village.' That scared me.

'David none of this is your fault.'

'Oh my God, you and Dad aren't splitting up over me, surely?'

'No, no! Don't be absurd. This is all getting out of hand. Anyway we're not splitting up; we're just going through a bad patch!'

It was no good. He stormed out of the shop, goodness knows where. Why did I handle that so badly? I had had no intention of going to see him even. And now I've upset him. Damn.

'How much is the clock, the one on the left of the three?' Some customer now assumed I worked there.

'Oh, I don't know. But give me a minute.' I could see a price tag dangling. Thank goodness I am long sighted.

'Fifty five pounds, sir.'

'I'll take it.'

Thankfully he paid cash. He looked at me a bit oddly as I didn't know how to work the till. Nigel appeared.

'Sheila! Has he got you working?'

'Well, he sort of had to go out urgently so I've held the fort.'

'Oh thanks, that's good of you.'

'Not really. I'm not sure how I've done. Probably messed everything up.'

He looked round the shop and then at the till. 'All looks OK to me. Did you need to get off now?'

'Yes, I will thanks.' I picked up my handbag and suddenly felt a strong yearning to go home.

'Oh, Nigel, when you see David can you tell him I'm sorry.'

'You're sorry? What for?'

'Everything. Tell him I'm sorry about everything.'

Chloe

The pink roses are a constant reminder. It doesn't help that I've cut a few stems and brought them inside. There's no getting away from it; Alex has made a gesture. A very simple and, dare I say, sweet gesture. Without even bragging about it he's made my garden into a little oasis. In fact I quite enjoy sitting out in the evening after work, however late it is.

But maybe it was David turning up that did it.

The answer phone must have flashed for a couple of days before I pressed the play button and his dreadful whinge about the antique chest and his prematurely pregnant wife was reeled off once more. I tried desperately to stop it, pressing every button I thought might help from delete to skip and even rewind but it was no good. Like David throughout our marriage it persisted on its course; undeterred and unrelenting. Finally it stopped and I felt exhausted. I pressed delete once more and it made the noise of a seagull being strangled and flashed an angry red light at me. I considered binning the phone and buying a new one but that did seem a little reckless. Thankfully the red light paled and I could only hope the message was lost somewhere if not erased forever. But that was nothing.

The following Saturday afternoon I was happily pottering around my house and garden doing all the things I don't have time to do during the week when there was a knock at my front door. My first thought was that it might be Alex and I felt quite excited and then I convinced myself it was the postman with a parcel that wouldn't fit through the letter box. When I saw David on the doorstep all the advice in the self help book 'Surviving Divorce' went out of the window. At least I don't think they recommend screaming at your ex or maybe they do, but only when he's not around and you have your head in a pillow.

'David! This is unexpected.'

'But Chloe, we have things we need to talk about. I've tried the telephone but you're just not responding are you?'

'Responding! To your ridiculous requests and your monologues about how you've moved on. Why can't you just leave me alone?'

'Chloe, are you alright?' Priceless! Am I alright? Clearly I'm a crazy divorcee with a ridiculous passion for antique chests and he asks me if I'm alright!

'Is this a bad time?'

I didn't punch him. It occurred to me that if anyone was to ever want to write a book on what not to say to your ex, here's your main source of material.

'No, I'm not alright! Don't you know when you're being ignored? You can't have the bloody antique chest for your half brained pregnant fiancée now or ever! Got it! You'll just have to go through the trauma of getting married without it!'

'Oh Chloe. *This is not you*. You really are overreacting and I'm worried about you now. I can see you're not over me.'

'Not over you! I'd rather sleep with a married man – even if he is the CEO of my latest investment! That's how over you I am!'

'Chloe, this is so out of character. Have you seen a doctor recently? Maybe counselling would help. You know *I've* moved on and *you* need to as well.'

'Moved on! I moved on two days after we got married when you started harping on about children! Why do you think it didn't work out! Now if you don't mind I've wasted enough of my life on you!'

After I slammed the door shut I realised I was trembling. I sunk to the floor, curled up and sobbed pathetically. In a while I listened and there was a heavenly silence. Perhaps I had even heard footsteps walking away. As the quiet continued I thanked God for this release and got up ready to fight another day.

For the next half an hour it was like I was on auto pilot. I decided on a mission and I headed straight for it. I daren't think it through, ponder the pros and cons or worry about the consequences. It was like there was a force within me I had no control over and whatever happened I'd see it through. I had a shower, put some make up on, brushed my hair and threw on a pretty summer dress. I managed to find a half decent bottle of red wine from my limited stash and as I swept next door my heart started beating faster. I did, for a second, wonder if I was going crazy but it was too late, I was knocking loudly on his front door, probably a bit too loudly but still there was no turning back. He took ages to appear, we'll probably 60 seconds and when he opened it he looked surprised and smiled from ear to ear.

'Chloe! Hello there. How lovely to see you. Will you come in?'

Suddenly I felt silly. 'I suppose you're wondering why I'm here?'

Alex hesitated before he said, 'Well I'm very pleased you are and I see you have a fine Medoc which I'd be happy to drink with you if you like?'

I then realised I was clinging on to the bottle for dear life.

'Oh yes, but only if you've time, I mean its Saturday evening, maybe you have plans?'

'No plans. And if I did I'd postpone them to make time for you, Chloe.'

Why was he being so nice?

'So, the bottle.' He was reaching out for it now and looking hopeful.

'Oh yes!' I somehow managed to release it into his possession. I realised my hands were clammy and thanked God it wasn't white wine. He wandered into the kitchen to find a cork screw.

'Do come through. It's a lovely evening, shall we sit in the garden?'

'Yes. Yes, that would be good.' Suddenly a light bulb came on and I felt a rush of relief.

'Speaking of gardens, the reason I came round was, well to say thank you. I mean for looking after mine. It really is lovely now. It's very kind of you.'

'Oh! You know about that now do you?' he looked embarrassed. 'Becky helped me actually. We just wanted to, well, tidy it up a bit for you. I mean, you obviously don't have a lot of time on your hands so..'

'It's very sweet of you. And the roses are lovely. I've been sitting out quite a bit actually.'

'That's good. I'm glad you like it.'

'Oh, I do.'

He stopped, turned and looked at me and his eyes were the most brilliant blue. And of course they hadn't changed colour but I suppose I was allowing myself to admire them for the first time. He didn't avert his gaze as he said, 'but I hope it isn't *why* you came round.'

Suddenly the truth felt naked. But actually it was a relief. At last I could be honest with myself and honest with him.

'No. No, I suddenly found myself with an irresistible urge to see you!' He looked up at me quizzically.

'Actually, I've had a terrible day with my ex, enough to drive anyone to distraction, so you don't take all the credit.' I smiled at him so that he knew I was joking and he smiled back. He handed me a glass of wine and I said, 'Cheers,' rather lamely. He looked straight into my eyes and said,

'Cheers Chloe, here's to us.'

Sheila

I watched George get out of a taxi and take his suitcase out of the boot. The taxi driver got out of the car and they exchanged words even shook hands before parting. It was weird watching him from Becky's window. Watching my husband return from a holiday he'd had with my daughter and granddaughter but not me. It was if, somehow, I was prying.

    He let himself into our house with a shiny new key, obviously supplied by the locksmith. Maybe the only one. Part of me wanted to rush round there and for everything to be how it was but part of me hated him. I felt all churned up inside and decided I had no choice. I picked up my key, the one to Becky's house now. Ringing the bell of my own front door felt strange and like it was a mistake that should be immediately put right.

    'Forgotten your keys again love?' he might have said.

    'Yeah, silly me,' I would have replied. But of course things are different now.

    He must have heard the bell ring the first time but didn't appear. He was definitely there. I hadn't imagined it. The windows were open at the front letting fresh air into a closed up house. The second time I rang he must have dragged his feet but at least the door opened.

    'Sheila,' he said lightly. He could have seen me and slammed the door shut. He could have told me to go away but he didn't.

    'George, can I come in?'

    'Yes, Sheila, you may. I've just got back from holiday but I'll put the kettle on.'

    I sat on the sofa in my own lounge like a stranger. I imagined him making the tea in the teapot with a blue design we've had for nearly twenty years. I could see him laying up the tray we bought at Whitstable with two mugs and a jug of milk and then of course the tea pot. I looked round the room to see if anything had changed but not a thing. He appeared, sat on the sofa next to me and poured the tea.

'I take it you still don't have sugar?'

'No, of course I don't. It's not been that long.' I wondered if I should have said that.

'No,' he agreed, thankfully.

We sat in silence and many conversations went through my head like, 'George let's forget the last month and go back to how we were. I can't bear this anymore.'

'Oh, yes Sheila, lets. This is killing me.'

And then:

'George, what's happening, I'm scared.'

'Don't worry darling it's all going to be alright.'

And then

'George, what now?'

'Well I think we should get divorced, go our separate ways. I've met someone else actually.'

'Do you want some milk in that?' I looked at my tea and realised there was no milk in it.

'Oh, yes.' But actually what did it matter. I felt numb. I couldn't taste the tea.

'Did you have a good holiday?'

'Not bad. Bit strange without you.'

'Oh!'

'What have you been up to?' he asked and I was thankful for the effort at conversation.

'Messing everything up, I think.'

'Oh?'

That sounded like a question. Surely he knew I'd messed everything up. But of course it wasn't just George.

'David's not speaking to me.'

'Oh, he'll come round. You two have always been close.'

I wanted to cry. At last some recognition of the truth. At last he'd said something nice.

'George I've hated the last month really. I wasn't my usual self when I went to stay with Becky. It just all got on top of me with David moving back and the tablets and everything.'

'Yes, I can see that.'

Was this a life line?

'You can? You can see I was mixed up? I didn't mean to leave you as such? And, well, Becky did need me. She was in a terrible state you know?'

'Yes, I've heard that. Poor Becky.'

'Yes, poor Becky. Puts our problems into perspective doesn't it?'

I was imagining all sorts. Being back in his arms. All forgiven. George embracing David and saying how sorry he was for not welcoming him back to Hartfield.

'Do you think we can work things out?' he sounded quite upbeat.

I let out a cry. A cry of enormous relief and gulped back the tears.

'I'd like that.'

'Well we can try,' he said, 'But things will have to be different, of course.'

'Oh, of course,' I said.

'Yes, you'll have to move back and Becky will have to manage without you.'

'That's not a problem, in fact I feel like I've outstayed my welcome.'

'And I don't mean to the spare room.'

'No, no, that was just the tablets.'

There was a pause and I seized the moment. 'And you'll make up with David, I mean accept that he's gay and welcome him and Nigel here in our home?'

George choked on his tea and his eyes nearly popped out of his head. He sounded angry when he said, 'I might entertain David. I want nothing to do with this Nigel person!'

The turbulence returned to my insides and I could think of many things I wanted to blurt out in horror but my mouth didn't move.

'I'm not having my son's sexuality waved in my face, you must understand that Sheila! I will take you back, I'll have a new key cut for you and we can go back to how we were with this little episode forgotten. But that's as far as it goes!'

I felt sick. I wanted to run and run until I collapsed and could die of exhaustion. The cold reality of my marriage with George engulfed me and left me suffocating. I now knew that I'd been desperately clinging onto false hope, deluding myself of the reality of the situation. I was shaking as at last I stammered out my truth.

'George, it's not going to work. Our marriage is over.'

'I see! You come round here drinking tea giving me false hope when really all you want is a divorce. You wicked woman! How dare you play with my emotions like that! To think that I was going to have you back! Get out! Get out!' He was bright red. That's all I can remember now. He looked like he might burst.

'No George, you've got it wrong. I did want things to work out between us but it's just no good.'

'*I'm* just no good! That's what it is! I just want to live by decent principles but you don't understand!'

'It's not that. It's just. Well. It just hasn't worked.'

'It worked for twenty four bloody years! Or did it? Was that all a lie?'

I was scared of him now. I picked up my key and almost ran out. Ran out of my own home. I thought he might hit me. But of course he wouldn't. And why did I shut the front door, but that's what you do isn't it?

I heard the teapot smash first. Against the wall. I heard the tea splash and the china crash into many pieces. And it stopped me in my tracks so I heard the thud. The thud of George falling to the floor. I shouted through the open window, 'George! George!' He was lying there. I screamed his name over and over. Alex appeared and squeezed through the window to get to him. He put his finger up to his neck and felt and then he grabbed the phone and dialled 999 and said 'ambulance' and then, 'Heart attack I think.'

'Not sure, can't feel it'

'Mouth to mouth...... OK....... Just a neighbour........... His wife............ Yes, I will.' He turned to me and then let me in the front door.

'Have you ever done first aid?' he said and I remember thinking how calm he was. I rushed over to George and held his head. I knew straight away he was dead. Still, I watched Alex take instructions from the person on the end of the phone and breath into his mouth and pump his heart and breath and pump and breath and pump and...

Alex made me sit on the sofa and drink a brandy while we waited for the ambulance. It seemed like an eternity but of course once they're dead there's no point rushing. I couldn't feel anything except the brandy trickling hot down my throat. I thought maybe I should be crying but every muscle in my body was paralysed.

'I'm so sorry Sheila,' Alex said. 'I mean, maybe I could have done more but I don't think so. I'm so sorry.'

If only I could have talked I would have told him that it was my fault not his. He'd been brilliant actually. But then I had to tell myself that it was just the way things were. A lot had happened and I couldn't take the blame for it all or I might never speak again.

Becky

Two funerals and a wedding. Not quite as cheerful as four weddings and a funeral but that's the world of films for you. I can't stand Hugh Grant, it takes him ages to say what he really means but still it's a bloody good film and I've watched it about 15 times. I cry every time when the gay bloke reads out that poem, 'He was my North, my South, my East and West, My working week and my Sunday rest..'
    You see George next door keeled over when Sheila told him their marriage was over. Poor George. Still, not much of a life spent mainly in a shed I think and him and Sheila really weren't getting on. And at least now Sheila's been able to move back home. As for the wedding, well, there isn't a wedding. I just like to think that Alex and Chloe might get married one day now they've stopped pretending to ignore each other.

    Mrs R was in her coffin in the front room. I've never seen anyone dead before. They'd obviously put some make up on her but she still looked bloody awful, sort of yellow. Any way one glance was enough for me and then I looked out on to the garden and I saw her in me mind pottering around like she did. That did make me sad because she won't be doing it any more.
    'She'll always be there in spirit, I reckon,' Alex said. He was looking out at the garden too. He'd driven me in the Bentley and bought white lilies out of company funds, he said.
    'Yeah, we better keep it nice for her. Exactly as it is now. She wouldn't want it any different.'
    Alex smiled at me and was good enough not to remind me that we won't have any say with the new owners.
    There were quite a few there, mainly from the village as far as I could tell and a few family who looked more worried than sad. Jonathan Morgan seemed to be the main man. He made a point of introducing himself and thanking us for joining

him in his grief. As Mrs R had never mentioned him I wondered who the hell he was. Frankly he looked more pleased with himself than upset.

The service was lovely and made me cry. Apparently Edie had chosen the hymns and had said she wanted to be buried in the village church yard next to Frank Bennington. No one knew who Frank was, only that he'd died a couple of years ago and Mrs R booked her slot just after the funeral. It made me wonder what he was like and what they'd got up to together and I decided there must have been romance. Then Alex pointed out that Frank's wife was on the other side, buried 10 years ago, and we both smiled.

When we left the graveside I was glad she'd been buried and that I'd be able to come back when I wanted to. Then it would be just the two of us. The after bit was back at the house. There were two old women smiling a lot and pouring lots of hot tea into proper cups with saucers. A woman wearing an apron put out sandwiches and cakes and looked at Jonathan for the nod that she was doing it right.

'This is bloody awful isn't it? What are we doing here?' It suddenly struck me.

'Fancy a walk round the garden?' Alex was good at making things better.

'Yeah, I do. And then can we go?'

'Of course, Becky.'

We did the circular tour just as Mrs R always did and remembered all the little things she used to say,

'Dahlias are particularly good this year.'

'I can't remember the honeysuckle smelling so sweet.'
'That oak tree is over a hundred years old, you know' and then at the end 'put the kettle on dear, let's take tea.'

I cried and Alex held me and gave me more tissues. We were just getting into the car when this woman rushed over waving an envelope in the air.

'Rebecca Wright?'

'I'm Becky, if that's who you want.'

'Doreen Mapleton. We spoke on the phone.' She shook my hand really firmly.

'Oh yes.'

'Listen I do need to speak with you sometime.'

'What about?'

'Edie Robinson's will.'

'Oh, she left me something, has she? That's sweet of her.'

'Tell you what, you know the King's Arms in the village? I'll meet you there in ten minutes.'

'No problem,' Alex said for me.

She was waiting for us in a quiet corner.

'What would you like to drink?' Alex asked me.

'I don't really want anything.'

'I would if I were you.'

I looked at him. 'OK, probably best, it's been quite a day so far.'

Alex was looking at the menu. 'There's a Cabernet Shiraz here. Should do the trick.'

I didn't argue. We sat in silence while I sipped the wine and it tasted alright although I wouldn't really know. Alex had a small glass of the same and said it was not bad for a pub. Doreen smiled a lot and looked nervous.

'So what's all this about?' I asked after I'd had enough messing around.

'Now the thing is Becky, Edie Robinson has left much of her estate to you.'

Alex spluttered and spilt his wine down his shirt and I wondered what an estate was. Maybe some kinda car. Seemed a bit odd to not leave all of it though. And didn't she know I haven't passed my test yet.

'She's left to you her house, and of course the garden and then after fees and inheritance tax, there's the princely sum of £210,000.'

'What do you mean she's left me *her house*? You mean that house is *mine*? *And the money*? What's the money for? Is that to pay for the house? What about Lordy Jonathan? Isn't he getting it all?'

The woman smiled and took a deep breath. Alex swigged back all his wine, didn't seem worried about his shirt and encouraged me to drink mine more quickly.

'The thing is,' Doreen said trying to be calm, 'the thing is that Edie was very fond of you Becky and she was very appreciative of all you did for her and well, frankly, no one in her family exactly endeared themselves to her.'

I didn't know what endeared meant but I couldn't imagine Lordy Johnny doing anything for Mrs R except getting on her wick.

'Well I don't know. I don't know if I can accept I mean I haven't got thousands of pounds to buy no house and..'

'But Becky you will be the happy recipient of £210,000.' This woman made no sense at all.

Alex leant over to her. 'Mrs Mapleton, may I suggest you leave us for a few minutes.'

'Well if you're sure.' She looked put out but went off anyway.

Alex went to get more red wine and then didn't say anything for ages. At last,

'Are you alright Becky?'

'Well I don't bleedin' know anymore. Am I?'

He smiled and then he said, 'the thing is Becky, it seems Mrs R wanted you to live in her house because she thinks the world of you and she wants to know you're going to be alright. And who better to look after her garden now she's gone?'

'That's amazing isn't it? But little me in that big house, it don't seem right.'

'I think it's very right Becky. You're a good person and you deserve some good fortune.'

It started to dawn on me what all this was about and I felt scared.

'But what about all the money?'

'That's for you Becky and between now and when it's your time to go I'm sure that money will be jolly handy, for general living expenses.'

Doreen appeared again. 'Have we made sense of it?'

Luckily Alex spoke to her.

'We're very clear Mrs Mapleton. I trust you'll be in touch.' He handed her a card for the Green Machine and at last she left.

'Well, what now Becky Wright? Your chauffeur awaits.' And he smiled at me and I thought thank God you're here.

'You know Alex, I just want to go home now.' And I just wanted things to be normal again at least for a little while.

'Lodge Lane it is,' he said.

Alex

Life is sweet.

The waiting was endless. Every time I ventured out of the house, would she be there? In the lane, in the village? Where *was* she? In Europe leaving any worthwhile businessman swooning perhaps; using that clever brain of hers to pick out the best green stocks; wining and dining in the City at Corney & Barrows with admirers looking on?

So when she suddenly swept round here and knocked on my door early one Saturday evening, I knew straight away. The urgency of the knock gave it away. It said, I've suddenly decided to give in! I've dreamed a thousand dreams and rejected many more either with a glance or a bloody row and now, well now, I'm here, no distance from my own home ready to submit to the guy next door! Suddenly it feels right after all that denial, all those reasons why not, I'm here! All of me. And might as well be standing naked!

Well maybe not naked. Actually she looked quite ruffled and it turned out her ex had been giving her grief and I suppose that was what did it. But none of this matters because for the first time in my life I'm in love and all angst has disappeared. I'm not sure if she is yet, I mean I think she'll take her time, be a bit cautious and all that but I trust it will happen.

She bought round a bottle of Medoc, rather good, actually and we sipped it in the garden, talking. Talking our truth. Laughing about the trip to Hever, admitting how we'd really felt, me passionate, her mixed up. Funny really, we'd been to see 'Much ado about nothing' and we were almost Beatrice and Benedick playing out the plot. Same sentiments, different lines. Now the play has reached its joyful conclusion and we relish every moment together.

Saw Freddy the other day. I said nothing at first which prompted a few questions.

'Everything alright old boy?'

'Marvellous, Freddy.'

'That gardening business of yours, going well is it?'

'Not bad.'

'What do you mean not bad? You're on cloud nine!'

I smiled. 'Court three is it?'

''Er, yes. I think so, three.'

It was as if my body had been taken over by an Olympian medallist, my joints loose, my muscles strong and the air thin and providing no resistance. The squash court was suddenly small. I glided, my limbs flew and I beat him five love. Shit. Should have let him win at least one. Just wasn't concentrating on the game.

'Sorry Freddy, I don't know what came over me.'

'You've shagged that City bird haven't you? Your neighbour. You've finally shagged her.'

I didn't answer except with a smile but the word 'shag' didn't upset me as it had before. Nothing mattered. I waited until I'd bought him a pint.

'I'm in love, Freddy. I'm in love with Chloe. It's not about shagging anymore.'

'You bloody are, aren't you?' It took him a while to take it in and given that it had taken me thirty years to find a woman who would change me forever, I thought that was reasonable.

'Alex, old boy, I couldn't be more pleased for you.'

We smiled and drank our pints and talked about nothing much and as we parted he punched my arm and said, 'Just don't shag around anymore, will you?' And as he said it, the very idea seemed beyond ridiculous.

I've been to two funerals in the last week. Quite bizarre really. And I'd witnessed the death of one of them. Poor old

George from number four. Bit of a strange set up there. He spent most of his time in the shed as far as one can tell. Maybe that figures. I found Sheila in a state of shock outside her own home, unable to get in it seemed. So I did what I had to, even mouth to mouth but it was no bloody good. I've never been with anyone as they die before. Sheila just froze. No crying, no words, nothing. It was as if she was paralysed and in disbelief. I gave her a brandy. It was her son, David, who suggested I went to the funeral.

'Would appreciate it, I mean, you were there at the end and all that and a neighbour. Did you know him well?'

Funny question. A son who didn't seem to know his father at all asking me if I knew him well.

'No, not really. We all keep ourselves to ourselves in Lodge Lane.' Then I remembered waking up in Chloe's bed that morning and then going round to Becky's to help her with legal stuff to do with Mrs R and realised what I'd said was a complete lie. But it was true I had never got to know George; just about passed the time of day with him.

'Funerals Thursday, St Mary's, 12 noon.'

'Can I bring Chloe?' It just came out.

'Who's Chloe?'

'A neighbour. Of mine and George's of course.'

So Chloe and I went in the Bentley. Becky went with Sheila in the funeral car and I thought how amazing it was after just a few months living in Lodge Lane, I was really part of it. We all were. Going to the funeral of the guy at number four.

Sheila didn't cry. At least we didn't see her cry. She looked like she was wondering what it's all about. According to Becky, her and George were about to split when he keeled over. It must leave you feeling pretty mixed up but she was clear about one thing.

'What's *he* doing here?' David had turned up with his lover, Nigel.

'Mum, he's my partner. He's here to comfort me.'

'David, please! Just this once. This is your father's funeral. Let's respect his wishes.'

'She's right,' Nigel hugged David before walking away. David wept like a child during the service.

Back in Lodge Lane I parked the Bentley up.

'Poor you.' Chloe stroked my arm. 'Two funerals in one week.'

'Poor me.' I wasn't going to turn down sympathy and any special treatment that might follow!

'The sun is shining and we need cheering up! Your garden or mine?' Chloe looked mischievous.

'Oh definitely yours,' I said. Now she was quizzical. 'More private.' I explained and she smiled.

'I have a bottle of Chablis, some smoked salmon and a box of Belgian chocolates in the fridge.'

'Perfect,' I said and we both laughed.

Chloe

Maybe I took my eye off the ball. Maybe I'm so happy being in love everything else takes second place. Maybe it's true what they say about how much harder it is for women to compete in a man's world.

Being neighbours it's all too easy to spend time with Alex. We've quickly slipped into habits: him appearing at my door a considerate half an hour after my return from work with the ingredients for a delicious meal and a bottle of wine that compliments it perfectly. And then of course spending the night. Our conversation is lively and fun, our love making passionate and heavenly. It all feels so right, so quickly. I'm in love.

In the meantime the European Green Fund made a gradual decline; such a gentle slope on the graph one could come up with plenty of reasons why and indeed, Julian, our Market Analyst did. In his reports he always ended with 'we expect to see this fund turn by the end of the month'. In fact, the way the companies I had invested in were being managed was poor in some cases and this was undoubtedly the explanation rather than trying to find any correlation with economic conditions. Éduardo Devereux was no exception and given that I'd recklessly slept with him after he presented his plan for improvements I had to be all the braver to tackle this one.

Then one day the fund took a nose dive. Confidence disappeared and the share value plunged. I'd rather have done a bungee jump than face the other managers at our weekly Euro desk meeting.

'Chloe, you're in trouble aren't you? What are you doing about it?' Robin held nothing back.

'There's been a downturn undoubtedly. I'm meeting with all the stock owners where there are management issues to ensure they turn the shares around quickly.'

That was the kind of response he would get from any male fund manager in the room, confident and positive without any real justification. Bullshit's another way of putting it.

'I suspect Nourriture Verte is top of your list. Wasn't it their CEO who turned up in reception asking for you one evening?' That was below the belt. It was 5 'o clock when he turned up and hardly my fault.

'Éduardo is well aware that I'm looking for a quick turn around.'

'Good to hear you're still on first name terms.'

I wanted to cry. Luckily he turned his attention to Mark on the International desk although this time to heap sickly praise. I went home feeling depressed. I even thought about phoning Alex and saying I wasn't in the mood tonight but before I had chance he appeared. When he saw the look on my face he just hugged me and made reassuring noises. It turns out he's been following the progress of my fund on the internet and knew about the downturn. It all gushed out over dinner. I even admitted to sleeping with Éduardo watching his face closely for signs of jealousy. He calmly remarked, 'We've all got a past and we've all made mistakes. Me included.'

I smiled with relief.

'Is he married this Devereux chap?'

'Of course!'

'Brilliant! We can use that against him!'

I laughed with relief and enjoyed his fighting spirit.

'Sounds like you need a European round trip to sort out all your investments. Give them a kick up the arse.' Alex was right but the thought of leaving him right now for any length of time was painful. I refilled our glasses and suggested we adjourn to the sofa.

'I've organised a couple of video conferences. There's some pretty amazing software these days, you know sharing presentations on screen.' Who was I kidding? I'd tried this approach before with limited success.

'You can't beat face to face.' Was he reading my mind? 'I had to do the Far East a few years ago. I did my homework before I went and worked out myself how *I* wanted them to improve, you know areas of weakness and all that. I even arranged to meet with some of the shareholders to find out what they were looking for.'

'That's a brilliant idea. They were mad getting rid of you.'

'Thanks Chloe.' He leant over and kissed me. 'So my, darling, would you like me to help you?'

'Help me?'

'Yes, I could be your undercover agent. You know, suss out the stocks, with your help of course, and together we put together a plan of action!'

'That would be good.' I said as if he's just offered to clean my car.

'Then we'll book the trip.'

'Right,' I said enthusiasm still nowhere.

'Two tickets, of course.'

'What?'

'Well, you know, I just thought you might like some company; a bit of moral support.'

'That would be fantastic!' I almost squealed with delight. 'But what will I tell F&K?'

'Don't tell them anything. I'll pay my own passage, sneak into you room each night and turn up at meetings as an outside consultant.'

'Alex Minter-Kemp, you're my hero!'

The next two weeks were hard work, exciting and great fun. Alex was amazing. So careful not to overstep the mark but providing heaps of support and doing lots of background stuff I never have time for. I even gave him access to my email so he could set everything up for me. Within a week all the meetings were carefully arranged. We were to see six of the companies over four days.

    The first was a small company in Brittany who probably had the least to sort out so a good one to cut our teeth on. Together we performed brilliantly turning on the charm and selling to them our ideas for change that we wanted them to implement toute suite. Alex even spoke fluent French, which of course is a massive help even though all those in top business positions can speak English. We drank strong café, not weak tea, we knew exactly what was happening in their industry and the wider economy so they had no wriggle room and had them desperate to please within two hours. We left with written promises but perhaps more importantly, a deep respect and desire to please L'anglaise. Victory! But as we walked out my heart sank. Alex turned to me.
    'Well done, Chloe you were brilliant.'
    'So were you. Thank you.'
    'It was nothing. Nourriture Verte next. Are you worried?'
    'Well, you know.'
    'Trust me, Chloe, it will be fine.

    'Ah Monsieur Devereux, we meet at last! Alex Minter-Kemp.' Éduardo looked disconcerted from the off.
    'You have brought a colleague with you, Chloe?' I realised then that as Alex had sent the email he had made out that I was coming alone.
    'A consultant actually.'
    'Oh that is fine, we were just not expecting this.'
    'Ah well, I'm sure there's plenty of room round your board table.' Alex smiled.
    'Well, of course. I was thinking we would have a drink first on the terrace.'

'I think we should get straight down to business. After all we have lots to discuss.'

'Do we?'

'Have you seen your share price lately?' Alex grinned in the most patronising way possible.

'Of course, I am well aware what my own share price is.'

'You'll be as concerned as we are then?'

'Shall we continue this discussion in the board room?' Eduardo turned to lead the way.

'Perfect!' England one, France nil. As we entered it was clear that Éduardo had produced yet another presentation probably full of avoidance of the truth tactics as before. He stood in front of his lap top looking rather nervous when Alex gave me the nod and I jumped in.

'Good of you to put a presentation together but actually we have some very clear thinking ourselves which we'd like to present to the board of Nourriture Verte. Where are they by the way? As you know I expressly asked for the full board.'

'Well, I suppose I could er...' He nodded to his secretary who scuffled out of the room no doubt to round a few up.

'Oh delays, delays.' Alex was loving this. 'And I have a table booked for seven 'o clock for the four of us.'

'Four of us?' Éduardo looked puzzled.

'Yes, Chloe and I, yourself and the lovely Madame Devereux. I thought it would be rather nice if we all had dinner together. Got to know each on a more personal level.' My jaw dropped. What was he thinking?

'Ah, unfortunately Madame Devereux is en vacances avec les enfants. This will not be possible.'

'Oh that's a blow. Still we'll make a threesome. It will be fun!' Now he's lost his mind. But actually it just served to unnerve Éduardo even more.

'I will not be available this evening. I have important matters to attend to.'

'What could be more important than this?'

At that moment the rest of the board shuffled in and Éduardo looked relieved that he was able to avoid this question from Alex. I was pretty pleased too. The thought of a dinner a trios was pretty appalling.

The rest of the meeting, while uncomfortable for them, went according to plan for us. It's funny but Éduardo was no longer attractive to me. That charming suave French man who had swept me off my feet had turned into a bumbling idiot full of apologies. Our tactics certainly paid off and the written assurances to take the steps we demanded were handed over.

The rest of the trip went like a dream and my admiration for Alex grew. The days were exciting and full of achievement and our evenings dining out romantic.

Within weeks the fund started to perform and the drastic losses were turned into healthy gains. Whilst I was pleased and it probably saved my career what was more important to me was that I now knew with Alex by my side I could achieve anything. I have fallen in love with an extraordinary man.

Sheila

So here I am. It's my own home but it feels strange. Everything is different. George is at peace in Hartfield cemetery. He won't be coming in from the shed for his lunch or his dinner. He won't want to know where I'm going or what I'm doing. It's just me now. They say in the quiet you find yourself. My quiet is deafening. Everything's a mess. Everything is my fault. Nothing is my fault. There's carnage all around me. There's nothing there. It's just me now. Suddenly I'm free. I can do whatever I want. I can start again. I can go on new adventures. I can travel the world. Suddenly I'm trapped. I don't want to go out on my own. The world is a scary place. I just want to curl up and for everything to go away.

If only George was alive. Then I'd be free. Free from mourning. Free from others' expectations of how I should play the part of the widow.

David took me out for lunch. He drove me about seven miles in the rain to a pub that he's been to before with Nigel.

'The food's good, Mum. Really good. And the house red's not bad either.'

'Great,' I said trying to be enthusiastic. The windscreen wipers screeched and dragged.

'Mum, you can't just sit in the house; you've got to get out more.'

'Right. OK,' I said not really knowing where I'd go. David didn't seem to be bothered by the windscreen wipers.

'Have you been back to choir yet?'

It was all 'back to', back to choir, back to dog walking, back to living.

'No, not yet, but the choir master came round yesterday and has made me promise that I go next week.'

'Make sure you do. What about your dog walking business?'

I'd never heard it called that before. We'd turned into a windy country lane and David had put his foot down.

'Yes, I'm going to start that again.' I'd had complaints from the owners but of course when I said my husband had dropped dead they said they understood.

'Good. So you're getting your life back on track,' he said.

I swayed with every turn of the lane not bothering to hold myself rigid against the movement of the car.

'I'm not sure what that means exactly. I mean I'm not sure what it means for me right now.'

'Oh.' He looked puzzled. Suddenly his straightforward plan of me getting back to normal wasn't so straightforward.

He glanced at me and put his hand on mine briefly.

'Mum, I just want you to be OK.'

There was a thoughtful pause before he added, 'whatever it is, I mean whatever you want to do, I'll do anything I can to help.'

'Thanks David. I appreciate that.' And I did. It gave me a glimmer of warmth in what had been a cold time.

'So what do you want to do?'

I had to smile, in fact I laughed out loud and I realised it was the first time I'd laughed since George died. David looked puzzled.

'David, darling, if only it was that simple.'

He laughed too. 'Well, Mum, maybe it is.'

It must have been the next day; I decided to walk into the village. I had the excuse that I needed to post a letter and I wasn't sure what stamp I needed under the new rules. The guy at the post office was always friendly and cheery but today he seemed awkward. I wondered if it was because George is dead.

'Fifty five pence,' he said.

'Does that mean it's normal or am I paying extra?'

He looked blankly at me and then, 'I heard about George, I'm sorry Mrs Gifford.'

'Thanks,' I said and felt awkward myself then.

I walked back out onto the street and didn't want to go home so I went into a restaurant called the Rendezvous. I'd only been in once before with David. As soon as I got in there I wondered what on earth I was doing. But then I looked round and quite a few people sat at tables on their own. There was a magazine rack at the entrance. A young woman smartly dressed rushed over.

'Madame, une table?'

'Yes, yes please.' I grabbed a magazine and sat down at a table in the window. 'Just a coffee,' I said.

She smiled. 'Café au lait?'

'Yes, café au lait.'

The magazine was one of those Sunday supplements full of young models wearing the most ridiculous outfits. There was a feature entitled 'Luxx hot list' with a man wearing a striped pink and see through plastic jacket. His nipples showed through and he didn't look very happy. It cost was £537.

The coffee arrived. I don't drink a lot of coffee but it seemed the right thing to do in a French café. I turned the pages of the magazine barely taking anything in. Whilst this whole thing seemed futile somehow I quite liked it. I watched the village going about its business and I thought this beats being in the house wondering what I'll spring clean next.

A man walked in and I recognised him. I'd seen him pull up outside the newsagents in a Mercedes a few weeks ago. I remembered him because he looked out of place in a beautiful tailored suit and he was handsome. Today he was more casually dressed. He sat at a table and read his newspaper. The waiter seemed to know him.

'Your usual Monsieur.'

'Please. Thank you.' Before his eyes returned to his paper he noticed me and smiled. I smiled back and then pretended to read my magazine. My eyes were fixated on an article, '10 Steps to Buying on Savile Row' something I have never done and am never likely to do especially when I read point 3, the starting price of a suit is £3,000.

I thought about changing my magazine for another but felt too self conscious to move. I watched the passers by on the street again and thought about ordering another coffee but didn't want one. I thought about ordering a pot of tea but then that would look silly, wouldn't it? Too many thoughts of liquid. It was no good I would have to go to the toilet. I walked across the restaurant as casually as I could but still felt all eyes on me. Of course they weren't looking at me, why would they? Unless of course they knew about George and were thinking, look she's sad and lonely now.

I fixed my hair in the ladies and felt like I was 22 again. I was convinced he'd be gone when I came out but he hadn't.

Suddenly there didn't seem to be any reason to stay.

'More coffee, Madame? Complimentary.'

'Oh thank you.' If was it free it didn't matter that I didn't want it.

I looked over the magazine rack, surely there was something better? Just then he appeared.

'Hello, erm, I hope you don't mind, it's just that I've read this copy of The Times and if you'd like it, well, you'd be very welcome.'

'Thank you! Yes, it has to be an improvement on this.' I said pointing to the magazine and laughing nervously.

He smiled.

'Coffee's good here.' I said and wished I hadn't.

'Yes, it is. Nice ambience. I always pop in here when I get a spare half hour. The name's Charles, by the way.' He offered his hand and a firm hand shake. His hands were pleasantly cool and large.

'Well, enjoy. Maybe see you again,' he said as he left.

'Yes. Bye,' I said rather lamely and feeling quite faint.

I must have sat there for another half hour. Drinking coffee, reading *his* newspaper. I decided that I'd come here more often. After all, as David says, I can't just sit at home. Then for some strange reason I suddenly remembered the money I'd saved up from the dog walking. I had no idea how much was in there. My dog walking business, that's what David had called it. I folded the newspaper, tucked it under my arm and headed off to the bank.

Becky

I didn't understand at first. It was one of those days which was weird anyway what with Mrs R's funeral and all those strange people. There was that cross one, Jonathan Morgan, then the solicitor, Doreen, who talked funny and came out with lots of stuff I didn't know about. But most of all, why would I? Why would I ever believe that I could be rich? I mean I'm normally wondering how I'm going to survive on twenty quid until the end of the week. Now I've got a bloody great house and two hundred thousand or something.

When it had all sunk in I was so happy I cried. I was trying to tell little Jack and of course, being two, he doesn't understand money and stuff. I thought about telling him he could have all the toys he wants but I don't want to spoil him too much. But then I thought what does it really mean and I told him. 'Jack, my darlin', everything is goin' to be OK. You and me, we're gonna be alright for the rest of our lives.' He burst into tears but then that was probably because I was crying too.

The solicitor sent me the keys to Mrs Robinson's house in the post. I don't know why but I decided I wanted to go up there straight away. Somehow I just couldn't wait and I wanted to go on my own so I got Sheila to look after Jack and instead of asking Alex for a lift I got the bus.

It was so strange using the big old keys to let myself in and trying to believe that this is my house now. I just stood there and looked around trying to take it all in. It looked different now with Mrs Robinson not there but all her stuff just as it was. The kitchen was all clean and tidy and the kettle just sat there waiting to be put on for a brew; the fruit bowl was in its place in the centre of the breakfast table but empty; the fridge switched off, the door left open as if she'd gone away for a couple of weeks.

The day room looked just as it did when I'd finished my cleaning and had tidied up for Mrs R. Her needlework basket, the television remote, just today's paper missing. Suddenly it felt warm and stuffy and I wanted to open the windows but they were locked. I found the key just where it always was under the big vase, no flowers of course, on the hearth.

The dining room and the drawing room were just as they always were hardly used, 'Just a bit of dusting and you're done in there,' Mrs R always said waving her hand in the air.

The stairs creaked as I went up. It had never mattered before but now it gave me the creeps. 'Creaky house for a creaky old woman,' the little lady said and laughed every time.

Her bedroom always seemed cosy. There was usually a hot water bottle at the bottom of the bed and papers on one side; but with the bed made up it seemed strange. I don't know why but I opened the wardrobe doors. Huuh! There's all her clothes still in there! You'd have thought someone would have taken all that away. That Doreen woman, shouldn't it be her? What am I supposed to do with them? Give them to charity, that's what Mrs R would say.

I counted the bedrooms. I'd never really thought about how many there were before. Five. Five bedrooms. That's ridiculous. What am I going to do with five bedrooms?

I went back to the kitchen, made a cup of tea – no milk of course - and took it out to the patio. It was drizzling a bit but I wiped a chair dry and sat under the umbrella usually meant for sun. The garden looked like it always did, happy, even in the rain. I just sat there sipping the tea and wondering what on earth am I going to do with this house.

I thought about selling it even though I don't think Edie would have liked that. Maybe I could make the new owners employ the Green Machine to do their gardening? I thought about renting it out, something Alex had said might be a good idea which I could do with his help or some kind of agent. But wasn't that as bad as selling? Then I thought about me and little Jack moving in and living here on our own and somehow that just didn't seem right either. And would I be safe? Safe from Eddie? I bet he'd find out, the papers have already been sniffin' round, and then he'd be over. Probably try and move in! It'd be a nightmare. It all seemed impossible.

    The bus home was quite empty when I got on; just a few pensioners except for a thin woman sitting on her own as close to the window as she could get. She starred out to hide her face. But then a load of school children got on shouting and pushin' each other around and filling up the bus. One of the boys had to sit next to her. He waved his hands around and knocked her arm but not meaning to. 'Sorry Miss,' he said and she forgot for a moment and turned round and I could see the make-up she had on to cover the bruising. You see I knew, because that was me once.
I caught her stare for a second. She looked scared. I wanted to sit next to her. I wanted to tell her it could be different. I mean look at me. But I knew she'd tell me to mind my own bloody business because that's what I'd have done.
    And then it came to me. I suddenly had the most amazing idea. I don't know if I can get it to work but then I never understood the gardening business to begin with. All I know is, if I can make it happen it'll be brilliant and make me much happier than livin' in such a gigantic house could ever do.

Alex

The knock at the door was so loud and purposeful I was surprised to see Becky standing there.

'Morning! You up properly? I need to talk to you.' She barged past me and went straight through to the kitchen before I had chance to answer and I thought what a long way this little lady has come in such a short space of time. As it happened I'd stayed at Chloe's and had breakfast with her before letting her go to work.

'I suppose you want that strong ex-presto coffee?'

'I'd be quite happy with a latte actually.'

'Ooh get you! Now you're all loved up you're drinking bleedin' lattes. Anyway I don't know how to use this bloody machine so you'll have to make it. I'll have the same. I'm feeling adventurous.'

As the machine did its stuff she sat at the kitchen table and fidgeted.

'Got something to tell me?'

'Yes.'

'Well?'

'When you're sitting down.'

I smiled. 'Right,' and having delivered the lattes sat opposite her in anticipation.

'You see what happened was I went to Mrs R's. On my own. On the bus. I don't know why but I just thought it was important for me to go on my own as it's my place now and I'd be there on my own if I moved in, well with Jack as well of course. Anyway it kinda freaks me out. I don't really know why but it just does. Being in that big place all on my own. But it was on the bus home that I worked it out. Well, when I say worked it out I just had this amazin' idea but God knows how I'm going to do it. That's why I'm here.'

'Right,' I said none the wiser.

'You see I saw this woman on the bus and well I'm pretty sure she's abused by her husband. All the signs were there. I should know. I was lookin' at me just a year or so before I left Eddie. An' I thought she needs help. She needs somewhere to go to get away from that husband of hers. A safe place. Then she could do it. Until then she's got no hope. And I thought Mrs R's place has five bedrooms so why not let her stay there. And then I saw the place as a refuge for women with husband's like Eddie and I thought how wonderful it would be if I could make it happen. And then I thought I wouldn't know where to start so I thought I'll go and see Alex. This latte's not bad is it?'

At that moment I realised I've become very fond of Becky. From thinking of her as a skinny little thing, single Mum who'd probably made mistakes, I now knew without a doubt that she's quite something. Her talent for gardening, her indomitable spirit in the face of adversity and now this. She's inherited a fortune and what is she going to do with it? She's going to help others.

'I think that's a brilliant idea Becky. And may I say I'm very proud of you for thinking of it.'

'Oh Alex!' Her cheeks reddened.

'Sorry, I didn't mean to embarrass you.' I said and was ready to go back to the subject in hand when she said, 'I'm not embarrassed. I'm just really chuffed that you think that. Means a lot, you being who you are.'

'Right. So we need a plan,' I said.

'Yeah, that's what we need, a plan.'

I got a couple of note pads and pens. Becky looked like a child expecting ice-cream.

'So where do we start?'

I started to think through the idea and all the implications it raised.

'Well, there are a few areas to address. I mean there's the legal side of things; would we be setting up a charity? Are we going to employ women to run the place? Will we need security? Can we get funding?'

'Blimey that's for your list. 'Cept I think we will need to employ someone to run the place and a nice big beefy security guard. He'll be the only man but it will be OK 'cos he's been in the police or something and you could trust him loads.'

I had to smile. 'Got anyone in mind?'

'Unfortunately not!'

'Ah well, you'll have to do the interviewing,' I teased.

'Too bloody right.'

'Then there's the issue of how to attract the women who need the refuge.'

'I was told about one by this nice policewoman. She'd been round after the neighbours had tipped her off when Eddie had been playing up. She was ever so nice.'

'Mmm. Good point. We'll check out the local police station, see what they think.'

About an hour later we both had long lists of things we need to do. We've called it Project Edie and I don't think I've ever seen Becky so excited but there was one thing I couldn't quite work out.

'And what about *you*, Becky? I mean where do you fit in all this?' I asked. 'Owner of a charitable refuge, yes. But what else?'

'I've decided I don't want to live at Mrs R's.' She looked sheepish and played with her mug and I couldn't read her mind.

'But?'

'But, well, I would like to move. I mean I'd like a place of my own so I'm not paying rent any more. Do you think I could afford that?'

'Of course you can! You're worth a lot of money these days. You could certainly afford a place like, this, for example.'

'Oh, this would be perfect. I would just love this place. Being in Lodge Lane as well. Where else would I want to live?'

I thought about the amount of time I already spend round at Chloe's and how I might end up living there soon enough but that was possibly fast forwarding so had to bite my lip.

'I'm sure one way or another you'll realise your dreams, Becky. In the mean time we've got lots to be getting on with and have you remembered we're due at Mrs Coldshaw's this afternoon. She's concerned about her Chrysanthemums.'

'She needs to get a life that one.'

'Or maybe not take the one she's got too seriously?'

'Yeah.' She was responding but looked lost in another world and I wondered.

'How do you feel about the Green Machine now you're a wealthy lady? Do you want to hang up your trowel for the last time?'

'Hadn't even crossed my mind.' She stayed thoughtful for some time.

'As long as it doesn't get in the way of Project Edie.'

Sheila

One thousand, nine hundred and twenty pounds. That is what's in the bank. Funny how it mounts up. And that's only going out twice a week with three dogs so if I did more.. Not that I need the money particularly as I still get half of George's pension.

But still it made me smile. The possibilities if I just spent it! George would have suggested putting it into some sensible cause.

'Well, we could do with replacing that window at the back.'

or

'Loft insulation is always a good thing.'

Suddenly I felt deliciously free. This is the first time in my life I've got some money which is mine and I can do whatever I want with it. I was flicking through a magazine at the Rendezvous when the idea came to me. Arianne, who I've got to know quite well now as I go for coffee every weekday, had brought over my latte with one of those little wrapped biscuits and we had exchanged pleasantries.

'How are you today Sheila?'

'I'm very well, thank you.' That's what they tell you to say in all these self-help books. Be positive and you'll start believing it. Don't actually contemplate how you really feel.

'We have just got this month's magazine, "Woman and Home", you like to read?'

Why not, I thought. 'Yes please.'

She even brought it over to me with a smile. George always thought such magazines were a waste of time. 'They're full of adverts,' was his summation.

As I leafed through it the women glowing from the pages all seemed to be everything I am not. I know they're all airbrushed these days but they look radiant! Their clothes are in beautiful autumn shades skimming their bodies. They manage to look as elegant in a woolly jumper as they do in a dress. When I got to the beauty pages there was much talk of the sloughing of apparently dead skin, moisturising for a dewy complexion and make-up to add colour and life. Then came the answer. An article featuring Pauline from Kent who had had a make-over courtesy of the magazine. They had sent her off to a spa for the day apparently for her well-being but as far as I could tell it was more about exfoliating and polishing her skin top to toe. Then to a top salon to have her 'dull lifeless locks' coiffured into a modern, easy-to-manage style. By the third paragraph she was having her colours done and off to Bluewater with a personal shopper to select her capsule wardrobe with the right garments for her shape. The "after" shot was a stunning transformation and, while I wondered whether or not the airbrush had come out again, it was certainly enough to spur me into action. I was inspired! And really quite excited. This is how I would spend my money.

Firstly I booked a day at this beautician's I came across in town.

'And what would you like done, Madame?' the girl on the end of the phone asked.

'Well, put it this way, I'm 55, my skin's seen better days and I've no idea when it comes to make up. I want the works!'

She giggled and then helpfully suggested a facial, body wrap, pedicure, manicure and make-up lesson.

'Sounds wonderful. Had I better arrive early?'

Next for my lacklustre locks. The guy that answered at John Frieda sounded like my son's lover.

'Cut and blow dry?'

'Well yes, but I might want colour as well and perhaps a deep conditioner?'

'This is a half day we're talking here. May I ask what colour you hair is, Madame?'

'Well sort of fair but going grey.'

'Right, I think you should go for the Deluxe hair makeover with Dan. That man can perform miracles! I've seen women looking like they've never stepped into a salon, clutching a photo of Jennifer Aniston and not being disappointed after three hours with Dan!'

I found myself laughing and loving the frivolity of it all. Surely I had nothing to lose but my drab old looks and everything to gain. Then I rang the department store in town and asked them if they had someone who could help me put together a capsule wardrobe for the autumn. Apparently Katie from their team of stylists was the answer.

After 24 years of marriage and being told I looked alright and what was the fuss about, I was finally doing this for me. Just me. I couldn't wait.

The experience itself was uplifting with all these lovely people saying nice things and the treatments all very relaxing. I adored my new clothes that gave me womanly curves and elegance; my make-up was subtle but enough to bring sparkle to my eyes and radiance from my cheeks; my hair now in a sleek chestnut bob was perfect. And when I finally returned from my last appointment and stood in front of a mirror to see the full effect I was overwhelmed. Was that really me? Tears streamed down my face and my make-up ran which had me laughing hysterically. I collapsed on the side of the bed and lay there until all my emotion was spent. Finally I am free. Feeling braver I repaired my face and make-up and braced myself for another look.

'Shelia Gifford,' I told my reflection, 'you're amazing.'

As I walked up to the Rendezvous, villagers took a double take. Arianne gasped when she saw me.

'Sheila! Vous êtes très chic!'

'Thank you!'

She looked at me trying to put her finger on what had changed. It's difficult when it's everything.

'It's partly down to you actually. Remember that magazine you gave me?'

'Ah yes. Well Sheila you are certainly a new woman now!'

I giggled. 'Oh but it's just clothes and make-up and a new hairdo.' And as I said that I realised that it was how it made me feel on the inside that was the most significant change. I felt wonderful.

Oh and Charles, you know who I met at the Rendezvous, asked me out for lunch.

Alex

Mrs Turnball's garden is a wonderful haven of peace. She has great oaks, ashes and London planes which have provided dappled shade all summer and now a wonderful display of yellows, oranges and reds as autumn sets in. The dahlias that edge the top of her lawn are magnificent and the jasmine has dropped the last of its delicate white flowers and is to be pruned. Becky and I have worked in silence this morning both deep in our own thoughts. It's perfect gardening weather, the rain last night leaving the soil soft so that the weeds slide out and the sun has kept it mild for us today.

I've thought about the French trip a lot. Chloe was impressive and clearly commands a lot of respect from the board members of the companies she invests in. As an outsider I was able to put the pressure on while she used her assertiveness to great effect. As a team we were winners and it reinforced how I feel about our relationship. But it also gave me a taste of what I've missed for nearly two years now; the cut and thrust of City life. At first it scared me. Do I want it back?

Mrs Turnball appeared on the patio with a tray of coffee mugs, waved and waited for us to acknowledge her before disappearing inside again. I called Becky and we sipped our hot drinks sitting on the wall that edged the lawn.

'You're quiet today.' Becky told me.

'Yes, I suppose I am. Well you haven't got much to say yourself.'

'Yeah, but you've got that look.'

'What look?'

'Like something's bothering you.'

'No, no, I'm fine. Just thoughtful.'

'You thinking about Chloe?'

'Sort of.'

'How can you sort of think about the new love of your life?'

'You're not deciding to move to France are you?'

I had talked about our recent trip to Europe, the wonderful food and wine and countryside. But she added defiantly,

'Not that I'd mind of course. I mean if that's what you want.'

'No Becky, I'm not going anywhere.'

'Well thank God for that! I mean, well, it's just that I've kind of got used to you being around.'

'You mean you'd miss me?' I teased.

'Well, yes.'

'You know Becky, I'd miss you too.'

She blushed. 'No point in going then.'

'No point at all.'

We finished our drinks in silence and then Becky said, 'so what are you thinking about?'

'Oh, I was thinking about how good life is and how I wouldn't want to change a thing.'

'Liar.'

I laughed. 'Actually I wanted to ask you something.'

'Oh yeah?' She looked worried again.

'Yes, you see the thing is Chloe has asked me to move in with her, so, I was wondering if you wanted to buy my house?'

Becky

I couldn't believe it! It was like the most amazing thing ever. I just threw my arms around him and hugged. 'Of course I want to buy your house! I thought you'd never ask!'

So when we got back that evening I just *had* to have a proper nosy round. I mean the place was practically mine so why not?
'Any chance I can have a look round?'
'Of course you can. I'll give you the guided tour.'
Then he went all estate agent on me and started telling me the bleedin' obvious.
'I know all about downstairs. It's upstairs I want to see.'
He called his room the master bedroom. 'Leave it out,' I said. But then he showed me another bedroom (would be good for Jack) and another! I couldn't believe it; Me, Becky Wright living in a three bedroom cottage in Lodge Lane.
But as if that wasn't totally brilliant he then says, 'Well, of course, you know the garden but you haven't seen the cellar.'
A bleedin' cellar. That's just magic! Jack's gonna love this, I thought.
'Wow Alex! Is this where the servants hang out?'
'Well, not in my world. As you can see I use it for storing wine mainly. Oh, and there's that old leather chair over there where I sit and contemplate life.'
'Wow, how do you do that?'
'Well you know just sort of meditate. And I think about what's going on and how I feel about it.'
'Did you go to classes to learn that?'
'No, no. Anyone can meditate.'
'I can't. How do you do it? Show me!'
Alex started laughing but he managed to say, 'There's nothing to see! It's all in the mind.'

'That probably explains it. My mind's not the same as yours. I've always thought that.'

By this time Alex couldn't stop laughing and I just couldn't help laughing too. And I realised that I was laughing mainly 'cos I'm ever so happy. Then he said something quite surprising. 'I propose a celebratory drink in the garden! What do you say?'

'Well we've certainly got something to celebrate!'

It was then that it dawned on me that I'd be leaving my beautiful garden behind and someone new would be looking after it. Only bit of that place I've really cared about. Alex asked me if I'd prefer red or white wine and I said white because I read somewhere it's more ladylike. He smiled as he took the cork out. 'You laughin' at me?'

'No! I'm just happy for you.'

We sat in the garden and I looked at it more than I've ever done before even though I had created it with him. It made me smile to see the cuttings from my own garden making their mark.

'Thank goodness you didn't put all that decking down!' I couldn't help saying.

'Yes!' Luckily he didn't take that the wrong way. Then he put his glass down and went all thoughtful on me again.

'You know, Becky, you're a wealthy lady now; you should really talk to a financial adviser and get some advice on how to manage you're affairs.'

'Can't you do that for me?'

'No, not really. I mean I can give you some friendly advice but if you're going to buy this place from me it all needs to be above board and all that.'

'If you say so.'

'The thing is, I've been thinking, the Green Machine is beginning to take off and we could really do with a vehicle. I've obviously got the Bentley and am rather keen not to sell it. If you were to purchase a small van or even an estate car we could use that for the business and you would have a vehicle for your own personal use.'

'That's great but one small problem; I haven't passed my test yet.'

'Well you can afford lessons now.'

I looked at him and daren't ask. It was silly really but he must have read my mind.

'Yes, I'm sure I could take you out in the Bentley.' He didn't really sound like he meant it but I took him up on the offer anyway.

The wine was going down nicely along with the sun and I was just thinking that this was perfect. But Alex had a bit of a frown on his face and then he said,

'You see, what you have to ask yourself first is, do you really want to invest in our gardening business? I mean with Project Edie going on; you're going to be a busy woman. You need to think long and hard about that.'

'But Alex, mate, I already have silly! You know, the day I met you I'd never 'ave believed I was going to say this, but I think you're one of the best people I've ever met and being in The Green Machine with you, well it's bloody brilliant. And gardening that's what I love! I'm not gonna give it up. After all you went through with the big City, I wouldn't let you down!' He looked ever so thoughtful for a minute and then he turned to me and said, 'thank you Becky. Now I know I'm doing the right thing.'

And then there was no more frowning just smiles and we raised our glasses to The Green Machine.

One year on

Sheila, Chloe, Alex and Becky

Sheila put the finishing touches to the garden table. It was covered in brightly coloured silk and as the centrepiece she had a sleeping Buddha lying on its right-hand side as they do, to prevent pressure on their hearts, so she had learnt. Too late for George. She allowed herself a moment to consider what George might have thought of Buddhism – stuff and nonsense. But for her this miniature statue evoked peace and calmness every time her eyes fell upon it.

She placed tea lights in the copper candle holders which they could light when the sun went down, if the party was still going. She hadn't seen her neighbours for so long, she did not know what to expect.

The weather was kind; it was as if they were having an Indian summer. Sheila smiled at the thought. She wore a turquoise sari which was striking with her auburn bob which she had had for a year now since her makeover or her 'new life' as she thought of it. The sun shone down on her garden and as she took a final look she remembered she was going to look out some paper napkins. Once inside she rummaged through cupboards and drawers and came across some of those tablets, the anti-depressants, she had once taken.

'Huh,' she said as she threw them in the bin. 'Won't be needing those again.'

'Ah the napkins!' She was pleased that they were bright red, as she had remembered; they would work well with the rest of the table.

Chloe arrived first, looking so relaxed and full of smiles that Sheila wondered if she was pregnant. But of course, Chloe had never wanted children.

'Sheila, it's so good to see you. It seems like you've been away for ages.'

'9 months; not even a year!'

'But what a difference it's made to you,' Chloe said. 'Look at you! Amazing!'

They hugged and both secretly shed a small tear.

'Where's Alex?'

'Oh, he's coming. Got back a bit later than he'd thought from a gardening job so he's just having a quick shower.'

'He's still gardening, that's good.'

'Yes, part-time though.'

'Oh? '

'Yes, he's helping me with my business as well now. '

'You have your own business? You mean you're not at FDK was it? In the city, I mean.'

'No,' Chloe laughed. 'No more F&C. Said goodbye and good riddance to them 6 months ago.'

'Oh wow! How wonderful. I mean if it wasn't for you, all those early mornings and airports, I don't blame you.'

The bell rang, and Sheila went to answer it. She returned with her son David and his partner Nigel.

'Can't believe it Mum, you look great! Don't you think so Chloe?'

'I've already told her. You're looking well too, David, and you Nigel.'

'He's been liberated,' Sheila explained. 'Life without his father's disapproval hanging over him has done him a lot of good.'

'I don't blame Dad. He grew up in a generation when being gay wasn't even legal let alone understood.'

'I'm sure he was essentially a good bloke,' Nigel chimed in, 'anyway, we always make sure there are fresh flowers on his grave.'

'Do you?' Sheila asked and they all looked each other and let out a giggle. 'I don't know, taunting him even now he's laid to rest!'

The phone rang just as Alex stepped out of the shower. He grabbed a towel, rubbed his face and picked up the handset.

'Is that bachelor boy turned loved-up country bumpkin?'

'Freddy mate, how's it going?'

'I've had better weeks if I'm honest.'

'Oh no, what's happened? You've haven't lost the lovely Jo already, have you?'

'No, no, still got Jo.'

'You don't sound too thrilled about it.'

'Yeah, yeah, Jo's alright. I like her a lot. Not sure I'm as loved up as you are though. Anyway, doesn't seem that important now I've lost my job.'

'Freddy, mate, I don't believe it! What have the bastards done now?'

'Oh you know the usual, cut backs, streamlining, only the crème de la arse lickers will survive. Stand up to your manager because he's about to make a complete fool of himself and you're out!'

'Oh that's dreadful. I'm so sorry mate. Did you get redundancy?'

'Yeah, the usual, enough to keep you in wine, beer and takeaways for a few months.'

'I'd come straight over but I'm just off to the neighbours for a bit of party.'

'You really get on well there don't you? It's like you're a different person.'

'Yeah, it's funny isn't it? My life has completely turned around and I'm so much happier. It's all so genuine here, no bullshit, just real people. Ok they might have baggage, be a bit loopy and so totally different to anyone you might meet at Oakdene or in the City but hey, they're the real thing!'

'Lucky you.'

'But mate they let all sorts in, you know.'

'Well there's a thought.'

'You going to be OK, Freddy?'

'Yeah, Jo's coming round in a minute, it's her turn for the suicide watch. Shall I pencil you in for next Tuesday?'

'Tell you what, why don't you come over on Sunday, come for a spot of lunch, bring Jo with you and we'll bounce some ideas around.'

'Are you sure?'

'Positive!' and then, 'Oh shit!'

'What?'

'I've just realised the woman opposite is staring at me through the window and I'm stark naked!'

Becky looked at herself in the mirror. It was the third dress she had tried on and she was still tempted to put her jeans back on. But Sheila had described it as a garden party and so a dress seemed appropriate. She put on the green one she had had on first and ruled out because it showed too much cleavage. She had put on weight over the last year. Contentment explained it, Chloe had said, quickly adding you look better for it. She let her hair down which had grown and was now expertly styled and coloured honey blonde by a hair salon in town.

'Bloody hell!' she said out loud. 'Is that really me?' She had to admit she looked okay and wished she hadn't rebuked Charlie, the security bloke, the other night when he took her out for a pizza after his shift at the refuge.

'Becky, you're a beautiful woman. You should wear your hair down more often.'

He knew how much money she'd inherited but actually, he was a really nice guy, treated her right and he paid for the pizza. The door bell rang and Janey walked in with her usual bag of toys guaranteed to amuse Jack until bedtime.

'He's watching his favourite film at the moment, so he's no trouble.'

'He never is, the little love.'

Becky had a quick look round the kitchen and noticed the back door was unlocked. How had that happened? Then she reminded herself that Eddie was banged up now. No need to be too paranoid.

'Back door's open so you may want to lock it later. Well you know where everything is, help yourself as usual.'

'Of course, don't worry.' Janey stepped back and took a proper look at Becky, 'My word, you look lovely, stunning in fact.'

'Don't be silly,' Becky blushed and grabbed her keys. 'Just in case you've nodded off; I don't know what time I'll be back. Is that OK with you?'

'You go and have fun, glamour woman!'

'Brilliant! We're all here now. I'm going to serve the champagne.' Sheila looked pleased.

'Oooh, what are we celebrating?' Becky asked.

'Well, looking around at all of us, I think we have lots to celebrate. You know I've missed you lot. Had a fantastic time in India, something I really needed to do and loved every minute of it but you know being here, back in Lodge Lane, it's the best!'

Everyone raised their glasses and Sheila toasted life in Lodge Lane. They sat down to a meal of Indian delights with chicken biryani, cucumber raita, lamb korma and aloo tikki and palak paneer.

'Did you make all this yourself? Chloe asked.

'I'd have gone down the takeaway,' Becky giggled.

'Yes, I did actually. All except the naan bread, you need a special clay oven for that.'

'Well it's delicious.' Alex said. 'You must have really embraced their way of life. And I must say Sheila, what you've done, I mean building the school for kids who just wouldn't have gone to school otherwise, well, hats off to you. In fact, we need another toast, to the amazing Sheila! Welcome home!'

They all joined in heartily and smiled at Sheila. And Chloe asked, 'have you been up to the church to see George since you got back?'

'Ah, George.' Sheila leant back in her chair and looked up at the sky as if maybe he was up there somewhere. 'I've found my peace with George, now.' She paused and a tear appeared which she quickly wiped away. And with a quick shake of her head, she said, 'helps when they can't answer back!' and laughed allowing her guests to laugh with her and they all sort of knew what she meant but mainly were thinking how much this woman has changed.

The wine flowed and the sun shone into the evening.

'Anyway, you two? Sheila turned to Alex and Chloe, 'what's all this about a new business?'

'Ah well,' Chloe began. 'Back in my city days one of my funds invested in a small French company called Nourriture Verte. They farm organic and eco-friendly products in the Loire region. Well, let's just say we had our ups and downs but after leaving F&C they approached me about importing their goods into the UK and becoming a distributor. So to cut a long story short, we tested the water at French farmers markets in various towns around here and the products went down a storm. Now we're in two major supermarkets and have our own website. The business is doing really well.'

'Wow, that's fantastic.' Sheila topped up everyone's glass again.

'Yes, and the funny thing is,' Alex chimed in, 'Chloe's old firm always had it in for N.V. and now they can't work out why their share price is doing so well!'

Becky looked at Sheila, 'No, I don't really understand all this stuff about share prices either. I said to my financial adviser just the other day, you need to make it all really simple for me.'

'Get you,' Chloe teased Becky, 'financial adviser eh?'

'Well it was your husband who recommended I had one.'

'Hang on a minute, I don't remember us getting married.'

'Well you're as good as. It's been a year now, and you still behave like a couple of love birds.'

'So *are* you?' Sheila had to ask.

'You know you are amongst friends,' Alex smiled and turned to Chloe, 'when they start asking personal questions about your private life, I mean none of their business really!'

'Well, when you've been the one that's brought you two together.' Becky tried to justify her intrusion.

'How do you make that out?' Alex had conveniently forgotten the months preceding the romance.

'Oh, you've got a short memory, what about the pink roses we planted in Chloe's garden while she was away. And I was the one who had to put up with you when you obviously fancied her to bits but you weren't able to get together.'

They all laughed and Chloe squeezed Alex's hand, after all this was hardly news to her. She turned the tables on Sheila.

'Anyway, what about you, weren't you romantically involved with that guy you met at the Rendezvous before you went off to India?'

'Oh him! That was fun while it lasted.' Her smile said that there was more to tell but she was happy to keep it to herself. And anyway the moment was interrupted with the distant sound of the door bell. They all looked at each other, after all they were all there. Sheila was about to get up when Becky said, 'I'll go.'

She opened the door to a man dressed in chinos and casual shirt and with blonde hair that flopped onto his forehead.

'Hello, can I help you?'

'Sorry to bother you, my name's Nick. I'm just moving in next door and although I've only got a small removal van, there is this Bentley in the way so I can't get anywhere near the door. You wouldn't happen to know who owns it?'

Becky stared at him and he looked straight back into her eyes.

'Oh, yes. It's Alex's car,' she just about managed. 'He's here at the back with the rest of us; you see we're having a bit of a party. Sheila's been to India for nine months and she's just got back.'

'I see. And you all live here, in this house?'

'Oh, no. I'm at number two, since Alex moved in with Chloe at number one, you see I used to live at number three. Anyway this is Sheila's house.'

'Sounds like a friendly neighbourhood.'

'Oh yes, we all get on famously. Why don't you come through?'

So Becky appeared with Nick.

'This is Nick, everyone. He's renting my old place.'

They all got up and introduced themselves to their new neighbour and whilst the men shook his hand the women all saw fit to give him a welcoming hug.

'Sit down Nick, have a drink,' Sheila insisted and was already pouring him a glass of wine.

'Thanks, that's great but the thing is my van's out there full of all my stuff.'

'Oh, don't worry about that,' Becky said, 'we'll all help you in the morning. Now do you want some curry, because there is a bit left and it's really good stuff. Lodge Lane's finest, you might say!'

About the Author

Gill Buchanan lives in rural Kent with her husband, Tony, and cat, Gracie. She has an honours degree in Business Studies from the Middlesex Business School and after a frustrating career in marketing decided to set up her own business.

As the founder of Hens Dancing her mission is to help women in their middle years to experience more of what life has to offer and to learn to dance with life. In her spare time Gill loves nothing more than sitting in a pretty spot, maybe a cafe, and scribbling away to create her next novel.

To find out more go to: www.hensdancing.com

To follow Gill on Twitter: @hens_danicng